A GOD NAMED SMITH

By
HENRY SLESAR

I0541527

ARMCHAIR FICTION
PO Box 4369, Medford, Oregon 97504

*For more information about Armchair Books and products, visit our
website at…*

www.armchairfiction.com

Or email us at…

armchairfiction@yahoo.com

—WANTED—
ONE MILLION SUPERIOR MEN AND WOMEN

If you believe you have superior and/or mental capabilities, and are interested in joining other men and women of your caliber in the most important enterprise of human history, you are invited to write for full details concerning the establishment of a new planetary home for the human race. This is an unprecedented opportunity to begin life anew on a better world: a world without fault and without end, where Nature is subservient to Man, and Man subservient to God; where beauty and perfection are more important than hate or lust; where Man can live in peace and harmony and eternal Truth.

Send complete details about yourself to:

SMITH, INC.
Flushing Meadows, New York

FOR A SECOND COMPLETE NOVEL, TURN TO PAGE 73

CAST OF CHARACTERS

SMITH
Creating a new planet was no easy task. Creating new life was next to impossible. Being the ruler of a world...perfect!

LUKE WINGATE
Getting the golden opportunity to be Smith's sidekick on the new planet was fine, but did he really have to worship him, too?

EVELYN ARMOUR
Ready, willing, and able—she'd dump you in a heartbeat if she could find a guy who had a dollar more than you!

ALITA MORGAN
This little beauty came to a momentous decision: the world would be a better place without Smith.

BURGESS
He was more than just a little upset that Earth was loosing its important scientific people to populate Smith World.

REV. HARLOW MOORE
He couldn't understand why the young genius would go to such lengths to memorize the Bible, then want to be a God himself.

"What Man can imagine, Man can do." A sublime premise indeed, but Smith thought of an even more staggering one. "What God can imagine, Man can do," he said. God built a universe. Could Smith do the same?

CHAPTER ONE

HE HAD a first name when I met him. He wasn't just Smith; he was Robert Smith or Ronald Smith, something like that. But in the incredible years that followed our first meeting, his Christian name was either lost or buried, and he became simply Smith. Not Smith, the Man. Just Smith. Smith, the God.

A thousand reporters have poised their pencils at me and asked about that meeting. I told them the same story every time.

"Well, there wasn't much to it," I'd say. "We were students at Ardmore University. He was the Boy Wonder, of course, only thirteen years old, and I was a sophomore of nineteen. But we hit it off okay, and became good friends. That's all there was to it."

That's what I used to say. It wasn't much, and it never made headlines. But I was shy of talking about Smith in those days. Now things are different. Now I have to talk, or the Smith-facts that have piled up inside me will blow up in some spontaneous eruption, and me along with it. I have to talk, even though there's a thin and icy voice in the back of my brain that says, "Keep your silence, Luke. Smith isn't dead. You can't kill Smith."

I was a sophomore, and I was no different from a hundred other wise-eyed young men at Ardmore University. We dressed the same way, did the same things, shared the same beliefs. Naturally, we were fashionable atheists. The only kind of Hell we believed in was the kind we could raise at frat parties. The only kind of Heaven we cared about was the kind that involved a bottle of 100 proof Irish and an obliging coed. We could quote you Voltaire and Shaw and Joyce and Nietzche. We thought the world was our oyster, but we were cynical about finding pearls in it.

I met Smith on one of my Hangover Days.

I was sprawled out on the cot in my room at the Psi Gamma House, clutching a No Parking sign to my chest, still wearing my best blue serge from last night's binge. It was Sunday, and I was content to sleep until Monday's classes. But I didn't. I began to sense that somebody was looking at me, so I pulled my eyelashes apart and peered out through the scarlet mist. A figure took shape.

"Pardon me," Smith said. "Is this Mr. Wingate's room?"

My eyes widened a little. Smith was something I didn't expect. He was a long-headed kid about twelve or thirteen, with a sad mouth and half-closed eyes and hair the color of dry straw. He was carrying a suitcase that was putting a strain on his thin arms and shoulders.

"I'm sorry to disturb you," the kid said. "But I was told to come up here. My name is Smith."

I groaned and struggled to an approximation of sitting position. I said: "Look, kiddo, didn't your mother teach you manners? Be a good boy and blow."

He stiffened, and his eyelids flew open. I found myself looking into twin caverns. Even in my sorry state, the sight of Smith's dark and empty eyes made me shiver. I said: "I'm Wingate, son. What can I do for you?"

"I don't know." He looked around the room uncertainly. "A fellow named Curtis told me to come here, see you about something."

"Curtis?" Gil Curtis was a barrel-chested senior, the class clown. It didn't take a slide-rule to determine what had happened. It was a Curtis special, the old left-handed monkey wrench, the striped paint, the phony errand. Only why the hell was Curtis picking on kids?

Then Smith explained. "It's my first semester here. I've been transferred from Crowley."

I pushed aside the No Parking sign on my bed. "Now I gotcha," I said. "You're the boy prodigy they've been talking about. Did Curtis maybe mention a left-handed monkey wrench?"

"Something like that."

"You're being ribbed, Smith. Curtis is Society's Funniest Man. He knew I was blacked out here, so he sent you up. You wouldn't have an aspirin in that carpetbag?"

Smith shook his head, and his tight lips made his pale face look smaller.

"I don't see what's so funny," he said.

"Neither do I. But no harm done." I looked at him with interest. "How old are you, Smith?"

"Thirteen."

"You must be a pretty bright boy. That oughta make you the youngest freshman they ever had at Ardmore."

"No, it doesn't." Smith turned towards the door. "I'm a senior." There was more than a tinge of superiority in his tone.

CHAPTER TWO

I didn't see Smith for a couple of weeks after that, until pledging time rolled around. We had a typically unparliamentary meeting in the frat house, and somebody mentioned his name as a candidate, half-serious, half-joking. Somebody said:

"You'll have to admit he's a novelty. And he's got brains. We could use a few brains around this dump."

"Why'd he leave Crowley College?" I asked. "And in his senior year?"

"Dunno. Some kind of trouble or other."

"Nuts," Gil Curtis said. "We don't want any runny-nosed kid around here. I say no."

We put it to a vote, and there was a limp raising of hands on the issue. For some perverse reason, I voted to pledge Smith. But I was the only one.

That same afternoon, I had the bad fortune to be walking in the same direction as Gil Curtis. He was loudmouthed and clownish as usual as he strolled beside me, and when he spotted the frail form of Smith coming in the other direction, his eyes lit up.

"Hey, here comes the egghead."

"Layoff," I growled. But it was too late; Curtis put out a beefy hand and laid it on Smith's small flat chest, blocking his path.

"Hey, junior," he said.

"How's the left-handed monkey wrench coming?"

Smith looked at him without blinking. "I think I've found one all right. I'm staying at the Ivy House, if you'd care to take a look at it."

Curtis smothered a guffaw. "Sure, Junior, let's have a peek. You coming, Luke?"

I said yes, and the three of us cut across the campus towards the auxiliary dormitory building that had been added to the University structures with the increased enrollment. Smith had a small, bare room on the third floor, and it looked even more cramped due to a conglomeration of electronic apparatus he had brought with him from Crowley. I surveyed the confused mass of equipment, and recalled hearing that Smith was some kind of scientific prodigy. I was a journalism student myself, and any gadget more complex than an electric razor made me want to lie down with a cold compress on my head.

Smith threaded his way through the junk, and picked up a shiny-new wrench from some canvas-covered object in the corner. He handed it to Curtis, and the buffoon took it in his right hand, an uncertain sneer on his face.

"Very funny," he said, hefting the tool. "You're not just a genius, you're a real comedian."

"Try it," the kid said coldly. He handed Curtis a large nut and bolt. "Take this apart. If you can."

I watched Curtis grab the nut-and-bolt from the kid's hand and apply the wrench. No matter how he twisted, the nut wouldn't turn. Finally, he took it off by hand and examined the screw thread.

"It's not the thread," Smith said. "The thread is right-handed. It's the wrench that's left-handed."

"A real comedian," Curtis muttered. But no matter how he tried, he couldn't remove the nut. His fleshy face began to redden, and his neck swelled.

Smith said: "I guess you didn't understand me, Mr. Curtis. It's a left-handed monkey wrench. That means you have to use your left hand."

Curtis glared, and switched the wrench to his other hand. When he applied it to the nut, it slipped easily off the bolt. He stared at the pieces in his hand, cursed, and threw everything on the bed. Then he stalked out.

I stayed behind, and watched the kid pick up his tool and put it away. Then he started fooling with his electronic set-up. There wasn't much expression on his face, not even a small glow of triumph. I said: "What kind of a trick was that?"

"Simple," he shrugged. "I just sent an ordinary wrench through a Moebius-warp. It came back in a left-handed molecular arrangement."

"Are you kidding?"

He stopped fussing, and turned his dark, empty eyes in my direction. There was a frozen hardness in his face that had nothing to do with his young age.

"Why should I kid you?" he said tonelessly.

"No reason." I shrugged and went to the door. Something made me turn back and say: "I hope you like it here, Smith."

It's hard to say whether the monkey-wrench episode was the beginning of the friendship between Smith and myself. It was a juiceless relationship; Smith wasn't somebody you could warm up to. We spent time together after class, and once in a while we'd go down to the coffee shop and talk. That is, Smith talked. Not about himself, but about the work he was doing, his studies, his plans for future research. It didn't take long to get the impression that there was contempt in Smith's attitude towards his instructors, and I began to realize that the student-teacher roles were hopelessly disjointed. Smith knew more about physics, mathematics, cosmology, and practically every other science than anybody on the staff, and there was an atmosphere of despair among the faculty.

Before long, I realized that my friendship with Smith was costing me the friendship of virtually every other student. I guess I was always an outgoing kind of personality, and it was hard for me to believe that I wasn't wanted in any society. But that truth was spelled out for me clearly. Especially when my own fraternity brothers sent a delegation to tell me my status. Curtis was the ringleader and spokesman, and he put the case bluntly. Stop hanging around Smith, or quit the fraternity. I got hotheaded at the crude proposition, and told them all to perform a freak biological act. Then I stormed up to my room and packed my bags.

That was how Smith and I got to share a room at Ivy House. And that was how I discovered the Bible.

It was a Saturday afternoon, and Smith had taken the train into the city to attend some scientific symposium or other. I was in my favorite position, horizontal, on the bed, having a cozy dream about a redhead. I woke up around two, and drifted around the room with the vague idea of reading a book. Usually, I passed up the books on Smith's shelf, having little interest in the jawbreaker titles that lined it. But this time, I looked, and with some surprise, spotted a dog-eared edition of the Old Testament. I lifted it out, and opened the first cover. There was an Ex Libra stamp that said: "TO OUR CHAMPION BIBLE STUDENT, FROM REV. HARLOW MOORE."

The first page read: *"The Holy Bible, translated out of the original tongues in the year of our Lord MDCXI."*

I flipped the pages of dedication to King James. When I came to the First Book of Moses called Genesis, my eyes went wide as I saw the penciled corrections on the text. Reading with Smith's changes, the first paragraph read:

"In the beginning Smith created the heaven and the earth. And the earth was without form, and void; and darkness was upon the face of the deep. And the spirit of Smith moved upon the face of the waters. And Smith said, Let there be light; and there was light..."

I have to admit it. Atheist as I professed to be, the sight of that altered page turned me cold and fearful. I looked out of the window as if expecting to see God's revengeful lightning crackling over the peaceful campus of Ardmore University. The fact that Smith had rewritten God out of the Bible seemed like the ultimate blasphemy, and I felt as if my very reading of Smith's revisions had entangled me inextricably with Smith's own brand of damnation.

"And Smith said, Let there be a firmament in the midst of the waters, and let it divide the waters from the waters. And Smith made the firmament..."

I closed the book and put it back on the shelf. Then I hurried back to the bed and sat down.

Was it some kind of prank?

I shook my head. If anything, Smith was humorless. Perhaps it was some kind of twisted vengeance Smith was taking upon the world; maybe it was a simple case of childish rebellion over a restricted childhood. Maybe he'd been tormented by fanatical parents, driven into a religious scholasticism, which he had secretly hated. The explanation seemed logical, but I couldn't let it go at that. I had to know more.

So I asked Smith.

He returned from the city at eight that evening, his small face showing that peculiar exaltation that any scientific conversation produced in him. When I made a casual reference to the altered Bible, his features froze again.

"Don't mess with my things, Luke. I've asked you before."

I displayed some of my famous temper, and slammed out of the room.

I spent a couple of hours getting solitary drunk. When I returned to Ivy House, I was singing a hymn at the top of my lungs. Nobody heard it; the students were all at frat parties or in town. Nobody but Smith.

He said: "Luke, I want to show you something."

"Show me what?"

"Something to do with that Bible you saw. I've thought about showing you for sometime, but I didn't know if you could keep the secret."

"Say, listen—" I said thickly.

"Never mind. Just look at this."

He walked to the corner of the room, towards the large object that remained covered by canvas. He whipped off the concealing cloth, and I saw that the object underneath was a tall cabinet about the height of a man, and four feet wide, the top half glass-enclosed, the bottom half studded with dials and switches.

"What's that?" I said. "Looks like some kinda coffin—"

"Just the reverse," Smith said. "Things are born here, not buried. Would you like to see it work?"

I shuffled up to it and pressed my nose against the glass. "Don't see nothin'. What's it do?"

Smith started to fool with the controls. The thing emitted a low-pitched whine. Otherwise, nothing happened.

"The glass encloses a group of noncondensible gases," Smith said. "Like hydrogen, and helium. There are dust particles, too, like water, iron oxides, ice crystals, silicon compounds. You can't see them now, but they're there, just as they might form within the rotating envelope of the sun. This device is activating those gases and particles at enormous speed, causing them to collide. They're being mutually exploded by each other, but are also becoming imbedded with each other's mass. Within a few minutes, you'll see them aggregate until the mass is visible to the naked eye."

My naked eye wasn't seeing so well, but I continued to peer through the glass. After five minutes, I thought I could see the pinpoint of something in the center of the cabinet. I blinked at it, and saw it grow larger. Before another ten minutes had gone by, I saw the pinpoint enlarge into a ball almost an eighth of an inch in circumference.

"What the hell is it?" I said.

"It's a world," Smith answered.

"A what?"

" A small planet. A very small planet, created out of an artificial cosmos. Right now, its heat intensity is almost great enough to shatter the retaining glass. So we'll have to start the cooling process."

He tugged at a switch on the panel, and I saw his small face go white.

"What's wrong?"

"The refrigeration switch is jammed. Something's wrong."

"Can't you fix it?"

"There isn't any time—"

I put my hand over his small fingers and tried to help, but even our combined strengths didn't do any good. I suddenly realized that Smith's anxiety was serious; I'd never seen so much emotion on his face.

"Still growing," I said, looking into the cabinet. I put my hand on the glass and yanked it away. "Ouch! The damned thing is *hot.*"

"We'll have to do something!" Smith's eyes were wild. Right then, he seemed like nothing more than a frightened kid. "If we don't stop the process—"

"Hey! Is this thing dangerous?"

"Get out of here!" Smith screamed at me. "Warn them! Get them out of the building!"

I hesitated. "There's nobody in the building. Just us."

"Then get out of here, Luke! There isn't much time—"

I took one look at the cabinet glass, and saw it begin to glow ugly white. "How about you?"

"I've got to try—"

"Nuts to that," I said, and put my arms around Smith's narrow waist, yanking him off the controls. He began to kick at me, screaming shrilly, while I tried to drag him towards the door. There was a hum in the cabinet that seemed to be coming from the expanding, spinning speck inside the glass, and I could actually feel the room growing warmer.

"Let me down!" he screamed. "Let me down, Luke!"

"Sorry, pal." There was unusual strength in his scrawny frame, and I remembered something I'd learned in swimming class. I cocked my right arm and let go a short, snappy punch to the kid's chin. He sagged unconscious into my arms, and I hoisted his light body over my shoulder. Then, with one backward look at the menacingly glowing gadget in the room, I headed out the door and down the stairs.

I was halfway across the campus when Ivy House was destroyed, in a shattering explosion that knocked out windows in the village twelve miles away.

The story of Smith's expulsion from Ardmore University is well known, and there's nothing I can add that can't be found in the newspaper accounts. The feature writers really had a field day with the item, no matter how hard the Ardmore faculty tried to put a clamp on the details. It was one of the standard silly season stories newsmen rely on: the scientist fooling around his homemade laboratory and blowing up the building. It was good for a chuckle on a lazy Sunday afternoon, and it served to confirm the popular notion that scientists, as a class, were a pretty dunderheaded lot.

It was on the day of Smith's departure from the Ardmore railway station that I first learned any facts concerning Smith's childhood. I helped him carry his bags to the train, but the 6:42 arrived late, and we got to talking.

His father had died when he was three, and his mother had been a solid, God-fearing woman who was frightened by her son's precocious abilities, and thought that a heavy dose of religious training would perhaps balance his intense interest in the sciences. His only contribution to that training had been his astonishing feat of learning the Bible, Old Testament and New, by rote, word for word. Thus the award from Reverend Harlow Moore. Then his mother had been killed in an air crash, and an uncle named Howard Cherney had been appointed Smith's guardian. Cherney had no qualms about Smith's genius; he immediately arranged for his formal education, and witnessed Smith's incredible progress through every school grade, leading to his enrollment, at the age of ten, in Crowley College.

Smith stopped reminiscing at this point, as if reluctant to reveal the reason why he had transferred to Ardmore in his senior year. But it was obvious that he had run into similar troubles at Crowley.

When the train pulled in, Smith turned to me and said:

"I haven't thanked you, Luke. I want to now."

"What for?"

"For my life, of course. My life is very important to me. Important to you, too, for that matter."

I gagged a little at that speech, but swallowed hard and stuck out my hand.

"Lots of luck, kid," I said. "And take it easy on the world-building."

"I'll know better next time," Smith said.

He got on the train, a pathetic and fragile little figure, toting a bag too heavy for him. I didn't see him again for six years, and when I did, he was well on his way to becoming Smith, the God.

CHAPTER THREE

On graduation from the University, I talked my way into a cub's job on the *Times-Express*. It was a nice little plum, and there were forty guys in my graduating class that were keening for the opportunity. I must admit that I used my association with Smith to develop the lead. My first contribution was a series of articles about Smith that rapidly developed into a popular series concerning other "wild-eyed" scientists. I knew I was feeding a myth, but my conscience didn't trouble me. I was a reporter; that was all that mattered.

After a while, the series ran its course, and I settled down into the real drudgery of newspaper work. It was three years before I could call myself a full-fledged reporter, and even then my assignments were on the minor side. I didn't earn a byline until my fifth year on the job, but when I did, you can be sure my circle of friends knew all about it.

Among those friends was Evelyn.

Evelyn was a fresh-faced kid only a couple of years my junior, and sassy as they come. Young as she was, Evelyn was already an accomplished actress, with two fat stage roles behind her. I guess I was attracted by the facts of her success more than her beauty; that came later. She had a lovely, impish face, wore her golden hair mannishly short, and had a star-quality in her eyes, a brightness that made heads turn in the street. I think Evelyn knew that I wasn't such a big-shot journalist as I pretended to be, but she also didn't care.

It was Evelyn who brought Smith back into my life, quite accidentally. I had been dating her casually, so had no real reason to take offense at meeting her with somebody else draped on her arm. But somehow, my temper got triggered when I saw her strolling into a restaurant with a man more than twice her age.

I called on her the next day, and began to ask questions.

"None of your business," she said, curling up on the sofa and looking mischievous. "I like older men. They have an air."

"They have an air, all right. And it smells like money, I'll bet."

"At least they're honest. They don't pretend to be what they're not. Howard doesn't, anyway."

"Howard who?"

"Howard Cherney, the man you saw last night. He's really *very* nice."

"And rich?"

"And rich. He's some kind of patent attorney, I think. From what he told me, he's worth something like eighteen or twenty million dollars."

I frowned at her. "I didn't think you were the type."

"Oh, don't be so moral. Can't I like a rich man?"

"Sure, but—hey, wait a minute. This guy's name is familiar." I chewed on my lip and tried to jog my memory. Finally, I came up with: "Smith. That's where I heard it."

"You mean that creepy college chum of yours?"

"He had an uncle named Howard Cherney. He became his guardian when Smith's mother died. The thing fits. Maybe the patents he's attorneying for are Smith's patents. Maybe my friend Smith is a millionaire now, too."

"How delightful," Evelyn said. "You must introduce me."

That was the beginning of my new relationship with Smith. Evelyn got the facts from her rich boy friend, and sure enough, he turned out to be Smith's guardian, a man who had made a fortune on Smith's electronic genius. He told her that his nephew was living in seclusion in a suburb called Harmel. I found out where and wrote Smith a letter. His reply read:

Dear Luke,
Will expect you on the 7th, at 2:30.
Smith

I expected to find something palatial, but Smith's address in Harmel turned out to be nothing more than a huge, poorly renovated barn. When I knocked on the door, Smith himself answered. I had no trouble recognizing him. He had grown upwards and outwards in six years, but his face still had its sad, boyish expression, and his eyes when they turned on me where dual caverns of disturbing darkness. He looked tired, yet somehow elated, inspired by a hidden power.

Our first greeting was hesitant, and slightly embarrassed. We didn't even shake hands. Smith led me inside the place, and I smelled an accumulation of dust and grime and ozone that wasn't pleasant on the nostrils.

"I've been working," he said, wiping his hands on his trousers."

"Understand you've done pretty well, Smith."

"I've done very well. I'm almost ready for it now. Another two or three years—"

"I meant your inventions. Evelyn, the girl I wrote you about, she says your uncle's loaded. I guessed that you must be fairly well off, too."

"Toys," Smith said grimly. "The only reason I bothered with the inventions was to get money for equipment. It's a costly business; you have no idea." He looked at me sharply. "How much money does my uncle have?"

It was a strange question, but I answered it. "I dunno. Evelyn says eighteen or twenty million. Don't you know?"

"No. I haven't kept track of the finances; I've been too busy. But I suppose I'll have to start thinking about money soon. I'll be needing a great deal."

"What for?"

He moved his lips in what passed for a Smith-smile. "You should know, Luke. You saw the original model."

Then I remembered the glass-enclosed cabinet, and the tiny ball of growing matter, and the dreadful moment at the refrigeration switch. I heard the terrible whine of the device in the soundbox of my memory, and then the deafening roar of the explosion...

"You're kidding," I said feebly. "You're not still messing around with that world-building machine?"

"Not messing around. Concentrating."

He walked to a door that led to the basement stairs.

"Come have a look," Smith said.

We went down the steps, and I halted halfway down to clutch the rail in amazement. Virtually the entire basement floor was occupied by a cabinet much like the one Smith had demonstrated to me at Ardmore. But it was wider; easily forty feet across, and some ten feet high. The bang of gauges and switches on the control panel were multiplied in the dozens.

I descended the rest of the stairs slowly, recalling the holocaust caused by the first device, and not wanting to speculate on the destructive possibilities of this one.

"Don't worry," Smith chuckled dryly. "A simple mechanical failure can't occur again. The machine is controlled by a servo-mechanism that's self-correcting. Would you like a demonstration?"

"No!"

"That's just as well," Smith said, and I sighed. "I've been putting the machine through a number of experiments today; I'd just as soon let it rest. Basically, the same principles are applied as the model you saw at Ardmore, although I've made some important improvements. I've learned enough since then to create not only worlds, but actually worlds with their own satellites, and in any orbital relationship I choose. My problems with the world-machine are just about ended, Luke. But I have a far more difficult project underway now—and I suppose I'm ready to concede failure."

"Failure?" I said. "That doesn't sound like you, Smith. What could you fail with?"

There was a tubular metal chair facing the machine. Smith sat in it, wearily.

"Life," he said.

"What?"

"Oh, not simple cellular life. I solved that particular problem two years ago, created a crystal grouping that was bio-chemically assimilable. I trust you won't mention this to anyone; I'm not interested in that kind of publicity. But that's the fact:

I've created laboratory life. The problem is to evolve it into something more than activated slime."

"I'm sorry," I said. "You're more unintelligible to me than ever, Smith. I don't know what you're talking about."

Smith pushed himself out of the chair and walked to the other side of the basement. He wheeled over an ebony-black cabinet with a high-powered microscope on its top surface.

"This will make it clear," he said. "One of my manufactured worlds is inside this cabinet; the microscope is focused to give you a good picture of its terrain—and its inhabitants."

"Inhabitants?"

"See for yourself."

I went to the microscope and put my eyes to the twin lenses. Smith made some adjustments for my focal range, and I looked at his manmade world.

It was a rocky, pitted, unlovely world. There were deep grooves and cavities and blemishes on its surface. It was arid and devoid of greenery.

Then I saw the thing coming out of a crevice.

It was sluggish, uncertain of its movements. It crawled with a clumsy locomotion of its gelatinous body, and seemed to be getting nowhere. It was colorless, and almost transparent, and completely revolting.

"Ugh!" I pulled my eyes away and looked at Smith in disgust. "What the hell was that?"

"A Smith-creature," Smith said wryly, perhaps even with amusement. "Nothing I'm proud of, you can be sure of that. But a Smith-creature nevertheless, created by Smith, nurtured by Smith, kept alive or made dead by Smith. But unfortunately, without the sense or intelligence to worship Smith, or make Smith proud of his accomplishment."

I didn't like what he was saying, and I began to move back towards the stairway.

"Don't be horrified," he said. "My meager effort isn't even worth that. It's made me realize that there is a limit to what I can do, in the time I want to do it. So I'm through with creating life, Luke. The project can't afford to wait so long."

"What project?"

Smith bent down and peered into the microscope. Then he sighed, and opened a panel in the side of the cabinet. There were four simple dials. He turned one of them, and looked into the lens once more.

"Farewell," he said softly.

"What have you done?"

"Smith giveth," he said, "and Smith taketh away…"

"You've killed it?"

"With simple heat. Like fire from heaven."

"You're crazy!"

I bit down hard on my lip as the words came out of my mouth. It was a thought I'd never permitted my own mind to have, and a thought I meant never to express to anyone— especially Smith.

But he didn't take offense. He said: "At times, a little madness is an asset. Just a little. But let's go upstairs and have coffee, Luke. We've got a lot to talk about." He turned and led the way.

We had coffee, and Smith and I sat around for an hour in the dim room upstairs, talking about our college days. I began to relax, until Smith put down his cup and said:

"I'm going to create a world, Luke."

"What?"

"A better world. A world without fault, and a world without end. A world where Nature is subservient to Man, and Man subservient to God. A world where beauty and perfection are more important than hate and lust. A world where Man can live in peace and harmony and eternal truth."

I stared at him. The pat little speech had come out of him without emotion. I had the impression that this, too, was something learned by rote, the way Smith knew the Bible.

"Are you serious?" I said.

"Deadly serious. Within two years or three, I'm going out into space and add another planet to this solar system of ours. The problems are vast, but not insurmountable. I had hoped to evolve my own breed of life for this planet, create my own kind of Homo sapiens by artificial evolution. I know now that this was only childish dreaming. Worlds are far easier to create than Man. Man calls for time; I don't have that kind of time at my disposal."

I didn't know what to say.

"I've calculated carefully," Smith went on. "I've worked on nothing else since leaving Ardmore. Now I'm almost ready to begin." He frowned suddenly. "Money," he said.

"Money?"

"You're right; I'll need a great deal of it, an enormous amount. You say Howard has eighteen million?"

"That's what I hear."

"It'll do for a start. Do you have any connections in the stock market, Luke?"

"No. Unless you count Briggs, the financial editor of the paper."

"It doesn't matter. I can learn what I don't know. My problem will be to develop a trading system, which will give me the funds I need without crippling the national economy. I don't want to inaugurate Smith's world by having a planetary enemy."

"Now, look," I said weakly, annoyed at this last expression of ego. But Smith wouldn't be interrupted. He fixed his eyes on my face and asked:

"What do you say, Luke? Will you join me in this enterprise?"

"What's that?"

"I want you to join me, help me. I know it's a great deal to ask; I'm sure your journalism career is important to you. But I want you on Smith's World, Luke. I want you to be by my side when I create it, people it, manage its affairs, bring it to a state of glory this silly globe of ours will never see."

It took me awhile before I could muster up the right words to refuse Smith's offer.

"You're being foolish, Luke. I'm serious about this world I'm going to create. You know me; I mean to do what I say. I'm offering you the opportunity to be my principal assistant. To be—" He paused, and his eyes stopped seeing me. "To be God's right hand."

I turned my back and went to the stairs.

"Don't decide hastily," Smith said. "If the scientific or spiritual aspects of my plan don't interest you, perhaps the materialistic will. If it's money you're interested in, I can make you the richest man of Smith's World, Luke. Women? You'll never have such opportunities on Earth as I plan to provide on my planet—"

"Cut it out," I said. "I don't want to hear any more about it, Smith. I suppose you know what you're doing, and I don't doubt that you will. But let's get this clear. I like the world under my feet right now. I don't want any other. And don't forget, Smith. I'm the old atheist, remember. I don't believe in God; not even your kind."

His face changed slowly, but it changed. For a moment, he was almost pouting, like a thwarted child. Then he was the Smith I knew: frozen-faced, sufficient unto himself.

"We'll see," he said quietly. "There's still time, Luke. Maybe you'll change your mind."

CHAPTER FOUR

Six months went by before I knew definitely that Smith's plans were beyond the dreaming phase. The realization came when Lou Briggs, the *Times-Express* financial editor, called me into his office and offered me a chair.

I was flattered. The *Times-Express* was an important business paper, and its financial chief a man of consequence.

"You know Smith?" he asked. Briggs was a small, sallow-skinned man with bad teeth. He looked worried.

"Yes, I know him. Why?"

"Been following the Wall Street news?"

"Not particularly. Anything happening?"

Briggs grunted. "Your friend's decided to take a flyer on the market. He didn't do so well at first; dropped almost a million dollars in two days of trading. We didn't play up the story; some of our friends on the Exchange don't like that kind of publicity."

"So what?"

"Well, he's been doing better. He's recouped his losses, and he's been gathering strength ever since. From what I hear, he's displaying the shrewdest trading sense since the days of the old Wall Street barons. The talk on the street is…" Briggs began to worry his lower lip. "He's out for a killing. Maybe the biggest in the history of the market. If his luck holds out—"

"What are you telling me, Mr. Briggs?"

"If this madman continues successfully, he'll cause a panic. There'll be millions lost. It's crazy to think that he'll succeed; the law of averages is against him; he's violating every sound law of finance—"

I couldn't prevent the snicker. "If I know Smith, Mr. Briggs, he's got the law on his side."

"Then you think he can do it?"

"I don't know anything about the stock market. But I do know that Smith's a genius. If he wants something bad enough, he'll get it."

Brigg's yellow face got paler. "I've invested myself," he said. "Invested heavily. He can ruin me…"

I stood up. "Is that all, Mr. Briggs?"

"Maybe you can talk to him. He's your friend—"

"Sorry. He's not the kind to take advice."

"Goddam him!" Briggs hit the desk with his fist. "What he's doing is immoral—illegal! We'll get the SEC on him! He can't do this thing—"

I walked out of the office, and my hands were so unsteady that I shoved them into my pocket. Then I sat at my desk and thought about Smith, and the more I thought, the more depressed I became. I was glad when the phone rang half an hour later, especially when I recognized the voice of Evelyn Armour.

"Hi, Sara Bernhardt," I said. "I was thinking about calling you. Doing anything tonight, or did your sugar daddy run out of glucose?"

"Luke—"

The choked quality in her voice took the flippancy out of mine. "What's wrong, kid?"

"It's Howard. Howard Cherney."

"What about him?"

"He—he was supposed to call for me tonight. But I changed my mind, I didn't want to see him. I called his office a while ago, and found out what happened... Luke, please come see me."

"I don't quite understand, sweetie? What's the matter with Cherney?"

"He's dead. He shot himself. Something to do with the stock market. I didn't think people did that sort of thing anymore—"

"Look," I said quickly. "Hang up the phone and stay right where you are. I'll come over as fast as I can."

I found Evelyn huddled into the corner of her sofa when I arrived, looking pale and helpless. All the shiny, theatrical brightness was gone from her appearance, but somehow, that made me like her all the more. Suddenly, she looked not only available, but human and desirable. Before we spoke, I took her in my arms. We didn't talk about Howard Cherney's suicide for almost an hour. We found other things to talk about.

I knew that Smith's invasion of the Stock Exchange was part of his master plan for what he called Smith's World, and I knew that he had been callous enough to put a down payment on that plan with the life of his own uncle. But now Smith and his ambitions didn't seem very important to me, not in comparison with the discovery I made that afternoon in Evelyn's apartment. My collegiate, sneering attitude about love had been radically altered in a matter of minutes, and nothing in the universe seemed half so important to me as Evelyn.

We began talking about marriage at once, I began to make plans for setting the newspaper world on its ear. I had a purpose and direction in my life suddenly, and I guess, in my own way, I was as dedicated as Smith was in his.

That's why the letter hurt so much, the letter that lay on my mail stack just two months after the Smith Panic in Wall Street.

It was short and to the point:

We are sorry to inform you that your services are no longer required.

H. Culver, Pres.
Times-Express

I went raging into the offices of the city editor with the letter, but all I got was a shrug. That afternoon, I spent four hours on the telephone, calling up every friend or acquaintance I had in the business, rooting out job information. None were particularly helpful, so I decided to make the rounds in person.

I saw the employment manager of every newspaper in the city. Without exception, they pleaded "no openings."

Evelyn was understanding. She suggested I try some out-of-town papers, and I followed her advice for the next two months. In all, thirty-four papers on the east coast, six on the west, and five in the middle states of the country told me the same story.

No openings.

It took me almost four months, until the year had ended, to realize what had happened to me. It wasn't slack season in the newspaper game. It wasn't my lack of ability or experience. It was much simpler than that. Somehow, for some reason, I'd been blackballed, marked lousy, struck off the lists.

"Smith," Evelyn said one night.

"What's that?"

"Remember what you told me, Luke? About the offer he made you? Do you suppose he had anything to do with your not getting work? He's practically a billionaire now. He could apply a lot of pressure..."

I denied her idea at first. Then I thought it over, and began to wonder. I sat down and drafted a blunt letter to Smith, putting the question in clear terms.

A day later, I got a clear reply, in the form of a telegram beneath my door.

It read:

YOU ARE CORRECT. HOWEVER GREAT EMPLOY-MENT OPPORTUNITY AWAITS YOU IMMEDIATELY. SALARY ONE HUNDRED THOUSAND DOLLARS A YEAR. REPLY AT ONCE IF INTERESTED

–SMITH

I showed Evelyn the telegram, and to my surprise, she began to laugh.

"What is it? What's so funny?"

"You are!" she said.

"You're dying to take this job with Smith, aren't you? You've always wanted to take it, really. I can tell from the way you talk about him. You're Smith's greatest admirer and you hate to admit it. You're not fighting Smith, Luke. You're fighting yourself."

I crumpled the telegram into a ball.

"Maybe you're right. A hundred grand a year can't be sneezed at. I couldn't make that much in ten years on the paper. With a salary like that, we wouldn't have to wait any more, would we? There wouldn't be any need—"

"No," Evelyn said. She came close to me.

"I'll call Smith."

"Tomorrow," Evelyn said.

CHAPTER FIVE

I was the first employee of Smith, Inc. to move into the 87-storey Smith Building that had been erected in Flushing Meadows, New York.

I suppose no building ever erected on this Earth has caused so much controversy as the Smith Building, with the possible exception of the Tower of Babel. Architects were enraged by its outlandish size and freak construction, at the way its curved surfaces twisted back into itself with all the hellish cunning of a Klein bottle. Economists were infuriated at the sudden drain of manpower it caused. Smith hired eight thousand clerical and stenographic workers in the first three months of the building's operation; almost four hundred of the nation's best programmers to handle his giant computers; three thousand engineers; six thousand scientists in every conceivable field; thousands of other skilled workers in assorted pursuits of industry. But undoubtedly, the most controversial aspect of the Smith Building was its function as a recruiting center for the superior race of Man that would inhabit Smith's World.

I still remember the first announcement ad prepared by Smith to introduce his recruiting drive. Many others followed, and a barrage of publicity that blanketed every form of communications. But that first ad is indelibly impressed on my mind.

WANTED

One Million Superior Men and Women

If you believe you have superior and/or mental capabilities, and are interested in joining other men and women of your caliber in the most important enterprise of human history, you are invited to write for full details concerning the establishment of a new planetary home for the human race. This is an unprecedented opportunity to begin life anew on a better world: a world without fault and without end, where Nature is subservient to Man, and Man subservient to God; where beauty and perfection are more important than hate or lust; where Man can live in peace and harmony and eternal Truth. Send complete details about yourself to:

SMITH, INC.
Flushing Meadows, New York

It's hard to say whether the first national reaction to the Smith-advertisement was shock, rage, laughter, or puzzlement—probably a combination of all. But whatever emotions Smith's recruiting drive provoked, it also produced replies. Replies by the thousands, and then replies by the millions. In three months, twenty-five million letters in all poured into Flushing Meadows, causing a major crisis for the local postal authorities, and necessitating an additional clerical staff at the Smith Building of almost five hundred.

Smith was overjoyed at the response, but his happiness was short-lived. The first eliminations of the letters left only twelve million. The first interview of candidates eliminated another three million. Then the testing procedure began, and it became apparent that the Smith-standards, as personally set by Smith, were far too demanding to produce the One Million Superior Men and Women the advertisement requested.

I had seen wholesale testing procedures before, but never on a scale like this. There were rugged medical examinations, physical tests so exhausting that they actually broke the health of many candidates, mental tests that were severe enough to cause breakdowns among even the most intelligent and stable.

Nine million people in all, motivated by the Smith-promises of Nirvana in their lifetime, submitted themselves to the grueling examinations.

After almost a year of testing, only sixty thousand candidates were marked "ACCEPTABLE" by the Smith-standards.

As for myself, I was given the title of Assistant to the President, paid regularly, awarded the deference my title commanded, stationed in a six-window office the size of a small railroad terminal, and given nothing to do.

It wasn't long before I realized that my function in the organization was practically non-existent. I had no talents that could be applied to either the formation of the plans for Smith's World, or the testing of candidates. My journalistic abilities had no place in Smith's schemes. Once, when I suggested that his World would require an historian, he nodded assent and had me recruit a staff of five of the country's most respected historic writers, and merely laughed dryly when I suggested that I become a member of their team.

"You do what you're doing," Smith told me. "We can hire all the specialists we need."

The answer depressed me, but I didn't argue. I knew that what I was "doing" was nothing at all, that my place in Smith's plan was to serve as his paid companion, errand boy, confidant, friend. If I dwelt on the thought, it would torment me. So I didn't think about it. I reported to work every day, shuffled meaningless papers on my desk, read a little, wrote a little, inspected the various operations of the building, and waited eagerly for payday. I convinced myself that what I was doing was justified: I was making money, and saving it towards the day when I could give Evelyn the secure life she was entitled to. When we had that security, I would leave this empty, purposeless job, leave Smith and his egotistical designs, re-join the human race and live the life that Evelyn and I wanted to live.

That was how I rationalized my life. Yet even as I argued with myself over its logic, I knew that I was becoming corrupted in Smith's service, that this easy life and its lush rewards were having a drugging effect upon my will.

Evelyn knew it, too. And one day, she told me her viewpoint in terms that left me no choice.

"I want you to quit," she said. "For your own sake, Luke. I want you to leave Smith."

I tried to laugh off her words.

"I'm serious. I was wrong to tell you to take this job, Luke. I—I didn't know what kind of monster he really was. He's sapping your strength. He's making you into some kind of jackal—"

I said: "Let's be realistic, sweetie. In another year or so, he'll have that manufactured world of his ready to be launched. Then the whole enterprise will be ended as far as we're concerned. We can take our money and live a little."

"Do you really believe that? What makes you think *you* won't have to go to Smith's World, too, Luke? He's so dependent on you—"

I laughed again. "Dependent on me? You don't know Smith. He's not dependent on anybody. Since when does God need a friend?"

"I tell you he is! In some kind of crazy way, Smith needs you. He won't let you go! But I need you, too, Luke. Don't you see what will happen? It's going to end up in a contest, a rivalry. And I have a feeling Smith will win. He always wins."

I put my arms around her. "You don't know what you're saying. Nothing could make me lose you, Evelyn. Nothing in the universe."

"Don't." She broke away from me. "I mean it, Luke. Quit now, or you'll never quit. Quit now, or—" She turned away from my eyes. "Or we're through."

"Evelyn!"

"That's how I feel, Luke! I'd rather lose you now than later. It would be easier for both of us. That's all I have to say. No more talk will help. You must make a choice."

The next day, I sent my letter of resignation to the head office. I didn't show up at the Smith Building. I told myself that I wouldn't take the risk of having Smith's arguments sway my decision, but I also knew that I was simply afraid to face Smith in this hour.

That night, I received a telegram.

ACCEPT YOUR RESIGNATION WITH GREAT RELUCTANCE. HOWEVER IMPLORE YOU TO PERFORM ONE LAST IMPORTANT ERRAND FOR ME. PLEASE VISIT DR. MARTIN CORCORAN AT SALO LABORATORIES SAN FRANCISCO AND DO WHAT YOU CAN TO ENLIST HIS INTEREST IN OUR ENTERPRISE. IF YOU ARE SUCCESSFUL WILL TERMINATE OUR CONTRACT WITH BONUS OF TWENTY-FIVE THOUSAND DOLLARS. BEST WISHES.
—SMITH

The reply startled me; it was nothing like the response I had anticipated from Smith. I called Evelyn and read her the telegram. She was equally dumbfounded.

"I guess one more errand won't hurt," I said. "And we could sure use the money. What do you say?"

She hesitated about saying yes, but finally did. I called the airport and made a reservation on the next westbound flight. Then I contacted the Personal Information Service at the Smith Building and had them deliver a file on Dr. Martin Corcoran to my home.

Dr. Corcoran turned out to be an extremely prominent biophysicist, one of the leaders in his field. He was a virile man of some sixty years, so totally immersed in his work that he knew amazingly little of the Smith-publicity of recent times. It took me almost a week to make contact with him, and still another before I could entice him away from his laboratory long enough to listen to an hour's conversation about the Smith-project.

At first, he was amused by my solicitation, and completely negative. But I had learned enough about Smith tactics to take the proper approach to a man like Corcoran. I painted a portrait of Smith's World that was a picture of idealized research conditions, a Paradise for the scientific worker, free of all materialistic demands, abundant in facilities and funds, ripe with opportunities for work and study. It was the right approach. Within another week, Dr. Corcoran was calling me at my hotel, wanting to know more about the plan, asking questions. The hook had been baited. By the end of the month, Dr. Corcoran was nodding his head yes to the Smith-proposal.

I returned to New York after thirty-five days in California, thinking gleeful thoughts of the bonus Smith had promised.

My first stopping place was Evelyn's apartment.

I had never seen her looking so lovely. She seemed taller, more ethereal. She had been letting her golden hair grow, and now it seemed longer than ever, spilling behind her back in a glittering cascade. There was a brightness surrounding her that was even more radiant than the hard star-brightness that used to shine in her eyes.

But when I held her and kissed her, I found her lips cold.

"What's the matter?" I said.

"Nothing, Luke. Why?"

"I don't know. There's something different about you."

She laughed. "Don't be silly. Was the trip all right?"

"It was fine; Smith will be pleased. Dr. Corcoran is joining the organization next month."

"Will he have to take the test?"

"I don't think Smith will ask that. Not for a man of Corcoran's reputation; he needs him too much."

I pulled her towards me, and again I felt resistance. Something *was* wrong.

"What the hell!" I said angrily. "What happened since I went away, Evelyn? You're different."

"No, I'm not. It's just that I've been—well, I've been so busy. Rehearsing."

"What?"

"I've been given a part, Luke. In a new play."

I grinned with relief. "Is that all? I thought it was something serious."

"It is serious. It's a wonderful play; the finest I've ever read. It's a chance like nothing I've ever had before, Luke. That's why I'm so on edge, I suppose. I don't know how to tell you—"

"Tell me what?"

"It has something to do with Smith."

"I don't understand."

"Right after you left the city, somebody from Smith, Inc. came to see me. It seems that Smith hired Arthur Trumbull, the playwright, to write a play about—about Smith's World. That's the general theme, anyway. It's a beautiful play, really it is, Luke. And Smith wants me to play the lead."

I stared at her. "I don't get it. Why you?"

"Why not?"

"Oh, I don't mean it that way, Evelyn. But what's the reason? Smith always has a reason."

"How should I know? All I know is that the opportunity is so marvelous, Luke—"

I didn't know what to think. I didn't like the idea, but I couldn't find any arguments against it. Smith had never demonstrated any particular interest in the arts, any more than was necessary. Was this some kind of public relations scheme on behalf of his beloved project? And why choose Evelyn, *my* Evelyn, for the starring role? There were hundreds of actresses with more stature.

Then I began to feel guilty about my attitude, and said:

"I think it's wonderful, honey. If Smith's behind it, the play's bound to be a smash. He won't let himself be associated with any kind of failure."

"I knew you'd understand, Luke."

I said: "What's the part like?"

Her eyes grew distant.

"I play Eve."

CHAPTER SIX

A month before the opening of Smith's play, the first Smith-rocket was launched from Death Valley.

It wasn't the first man-carrying rocket, which had left Earth. By now, the Air Force Interplanetary Corps had launched half a dozen manned vehicles on exploratory flights in the Earth's orbit, and two successful landings had been made on the Moon.

But the Smith-vessel, a sixty-rocket, 10,000-ton monster, dwarfed anything that had been previously launched into space. Its time of departure, its cargo, its destination, its purpose, were all kept under a security cloud.

Two days later, a second Smith-rocket departed, and days apart, two other ships left the Death Valley desert, heading out to join the other vessels on some mysterious mission in outer space.

I won't conceal the fact that the mechanics of how Smith planned to create his world in actual space mystified me thoroughly, despite my closeness to Smith. Perhaps not even the thousands of scientists now in his employ understood it completely, although many submitted learned articles on Smith's world-building process to their trade journals. I tried to extrapolate the method from what I had seen in the Smith world-machine at the University and his suburban laboratory in Harmel, but the problems of creating a planet away from those controlled conditions seemed so vast that my head ached when I thought about it. Vaguely, I reasoned that he would have to attract an enormous amount of interstellar particles to some central point, and recreate the conditions that took Nature billions of years to produce in an incredibly abbreviated time. The task seemed impossible. But I knew Smith.

Then the play opened.

Few of us who were there will ever forget that first performance of Arthur Trumbull's *The World*. On the surface, it seemed no different from a hundred other first-nights on Broadway, but there was a tangible air of special excitement the moment the audience faced the gigantic curtain in the city's largest theatre. No backstage visitors were permitted, so I didn't get the chance to see Evelyn before curtain time. I took my seat in the fifth row, and studied the program notes.

Then Smith came in.

His arrival created a reaction on that audience such as no stage performance could have equaled. When he took his seat down front, every head turned to see the man whose genius was at this very moment creating a new planet for the solar system.

He nodded to me briefly before sitting down, and the nod brought awed and curious glances in my direction. I stirred uncomfortably, trying not to feel pleased at this tribute.

Then the curtain rose.

You've probably seen *The World,* or read it in book form, and you know its merits and faults as a work of theatrical fiction. Perhaps you were even fortunate enough to see Evelyn Armour in the role of Eve. But unless you were among the audience on that opening night, you can't imagine the intensity of emotion that play or that performance could generate in the human soul.

Some critics call *The World* a religious play, and I suppose with some truth. But only those who knew Smith as I did realized the deeper significance of the play's action, the terrible meaning concealed in the glib, poetic dialogue. For as I watched the stage, I knew that Smith had subtly guided Trumbull's efforts in a manner calculated not to praise the God of our Fathers, the God of Sinai or Judah, the God of Calvary, the God of Jesus; the God of the Jews or Christians or Moslems, or any other religion, creed, or sect. There was only one God to whom the words on the stage were directed.

Smith.

Smith, the God.

Evelyn's performance was brilliant. Her radiance seemed to light the stage with evangelical fire. But somehow, I couldn't merely feel proud of her. I felt afraid, too, as if the role she was playing was more truly herself than the Evelyn I knew.

The curtain descended to thunderous applause, and when the house lights returned, I saw that Smith was no longer in his seat.

I tried to reach Evelyn backstage, but the attempt failed. I went out into the street and spent three hours at a neighboring bar, getting thoroughly stoned. Then I went up to her apartment, and pushed open the door without knocking.

"Luke—"

She turned to me, and her eyes were wide and frightened over the shoulder of the man who was holding her in his arms.

I felt nothing; not rage, not injury, nothing.

"I'm sorry," Smith said quietly. "I'm really very sorry, Luke."

"It's nothing," I muttered stupidly. "Think nothing of it."

Evelyn began to cry, and Smith comforted her.

"It's all right," I said. "Really, Evelyn, it's all right. I understand."

Then the numbness passed, and an emotion too complex for me to name swept through me.

I dropped to my knees and folded my hands beneath my chin.

"Thank you, O Lord," I said. "Thank you for all our many blessings." Once I began I couldn't stop.

Smith said: "Get up, Luke."

"Smith is my shepherd, I shall not want…"

"You're drunk," Smith said coldly. "Get up and go to bed, Luke. We can talk about this tomorrow."

"All hail," I said, and ridiculously, there were tears in my eyes. "Hail to our Lord Smith, God of the Universe, Lord of all Creation. Praise Smith unto the Highest..."

Then I fell forward, grateful that I had drunk enough to be rewarded with oblivion.

CHAPTER SEVEN

The year that followed is a year I don't like to remember, and a year in which the events following the launching of the Smith-rockets into outer space were public knowledge. You know the basic facts, of course. The fact that Smith's World, a planet the size of Mercury, 3,000 miles in diameter, provided with an atmosphere perhaps even more favorable for the sustainment of life than our own, became part of the orbital pattern of the solar system, equidistant to Earth and the planet Mars.

You know that the exodus from Earth to Smith's World was coincided with one of the most disastrous economic panics in the nation's history. You know the story of the east coast riots, and the unsuccessful attempt to indict Smith on the charge of high treason. The whole incredible tale of that year that has been chronicled many times, and by journalists better equipped than myself to detail them.

It was a year of Hell for many people. It was a year of Hell for myself.

There's one thing I wish to make clear. Without understanding of this point, this whole recording of my Smith-facts loses meaning. The year that I spent in the sanitarium at Boonsocket had nothing whatever to do with the health of my mind, not in any pathological sense. That's a fact that can be verified. I became a simon-pure alcoholic; there was never any question about my sanity.

Nor should there be any doubt as to whether my stay in the sanitarium was voluntary or not. It was; Smith had nothing to do with it. After Evelyn made her decision to join Smith on his World, I sought my solace in the brown bottle and found it waiting for me there. I drank myself into that sanitarium; there was no effort on Smith's part to have me put away. On the contrary—Smith continued to make overtures to me, offerings of money and other help. It seems he never forgot the obligation he felt towards me, because of what happened that night of the explosion at Ardmore University. Say what you will of Smith. He was grateful to me.

I was in the sanitarium for nine months, before I was able to re-enter the outside world.

It was a different world I found. A quieter, more humble world, a world no longer certain of its superiority in the cosmos.

There was no news from Smith's world.

A few tales would trickle in but nothing noteworthy.

After a while, I found a job. It wasn't much of a job: I became the assistant editor on a low-circulation picture magazine that probably hired me in the hope I would someday give them the rights to the Smith-story as I knew it. They didn't press me for it; they were content to wait. But I was trying hard to forget everything about Smith, particularly as he concerned Evelyn. I knew now that Smith's seduction of Evelyn had begun merely as an attempt to remove her influence from me, so that I would continue as Smith's paid companion without interference. Then the seduction had become something else, and Smith had found a Queen for his new kingdom.

But I didn't think about it.

I did my job conscientiously, if not brilliantly. The large amount of money I had earned in Smith's employ had dwindled as a result of my alcoholic year, and I needed the dollars that came in my pay envelope every two weeks.

I took a small room in a boarding house in a moderate section of the city. I kept regular hours, had few friends, and slept a great deal.

That was the only time I was unable to keep Smith out of my mind: when sleep came. Because sleep brought dreams, and my dreams brought me a vision of Smith that was repeated without variation; night after night the same thing appeared.

I would see the panorama of space, the star-studded blackness of the void, awesome and mighty and beautiful.

Then I would see a great spaceship leaving the green planet, which was its home, a spaceship throbbing with the humanity inside it.

At first, the ship remained evenly on its course, heading for some rendezvous with a better world.

Then the hand would appeal.

A giant hand, the hand of a God, fingers galaxy-sized would reach forth towards the spaceship, as if dissatisfied with its destination.

Then the fingers would close slowly around the vessel, slowly encircle it, hold it in its palm, crush it, destroy it.

It was the hand of Smith. I knew it could be no other.

But except for that dream, my conscious mind knew nothing of Smith. It wasn't Smith that troubled my waking hours. It was someone else.

And every evening, I'd look out of my window and see the pinpoint of light in the heavens that was Smith's World, and I would fight off my thoughts of Evelyn.

Then the Ghost came.

I was sleeping when it arrived, and when its hoarse voice awakened me, I thought that the delirium of drink which had plagued me months before had returned.

The Ghost was standing at the foot of my bed, shimmering as if in waves of heat, staring at me with hollow eyes.

I wanted to scream, but my throat was dry.

Then I recognized the uncertain form.

It was Smith. The Ghost of Smith.

"Luke," the hoarse voice said, a grating distortion of Smith's own mellow tones.

"Who are you?" I said.

"You know me. I am Smith. Don't be frightened; this is no mumbo-jumbo, Luke. This is Smith, your friend."

"Listen to me," the Ghost said. "You are not seeing phantoms. This is merely an electronic projection of my own image, a purely mechanical trick. I'm not quite sure how I appear to you; the device is still imperfect."

"Where are you?"

"I am on Smith's World, in my own chambers. This is the first such projection I have made, and it is not a complete success. I am unable to see you clearly, Luke. If you can see and understand me, please signify."

"Yes," I said. "I can understand you. What do you want?"

"Only to talk to you, Luke. I understand that you haven't been well. I'm sorry."

I snorted.

"You are still angry with me over Evelyn. I'm sorry for that, too, Luke. But we have no time for apologies; this contact may be broken at any moment. I wish to ask you to join us on Smith's World."

"Never," I said. "You're wasting your time, Smith. I don't want any part of it."

"You must think it over, Luke. Let me tell you about what my world is like. It is a world of perfection. A world of alabaster cities and human harmony. A world of beauty. Look at me, Luke. Can you see what I am holding?"

The Ghost lifted something round in its hand. I couldn't make it out.

"It's an apple, an apple straight from a new Garden of Eden, twelve inches in diameter. And not one of your monstrous chemical grown fruits, Luke. A tender, juicy apple, typical of our farm produce, symbolic of the difference between the old world and the new. Our grass and trees are the greenest you have ever seen, Luke. Our waters are clear as mirrors, and our weather is the balmiest you have ever known. There are birds of rarest beauty, and wild life of exquisite perfection. Our cities are wonders, and our culture is already a thriving, vital thing. It is Heaven, Luke."

"Go away!" I buried my face in the pillows.

"I want you on Smith's World, Luke. You will be happy here. There are women of extraordinary loveliness who want you here."

I said: "How is Evelyn?"

The Smith-Ghost said nothing.

Then: "I'm offering you Paradise, Luke. Will you refuse me for the sake of Evelyn alone? Is that the one factor which makes you say no?"

"Yes," I said angrily. "I'm sorry if it seems trivial to you, Smith. But that's how I feel, and I say the hell with you!"

"Then you refuse?"

"Yes!" I shouted. "I refuse! I won't worship you, Smith! You're not my God!"

"Do you have a God?"

"Maybe I do." My voice trembled. "Maybe you've made me see God, Smith. Maybe you've converted me, all by yourself. Imagine that!" I started to laugh. "You make me want to pray, Smith, pray to the God of Earth. And if I do, I'll mention you in my prayers. I'll ask forgiveness for you, Smith, forgiveness…"

I couldn't stop the sobs that came into my throat.

"I'm sorry," Smith said gently.

The Ghost vanished.

CHAPTER EIGHT

I suppose that was the first contact Smith made with Earth since his departure. But it wasn't his last. Five months after the Ghost's visit to my bedroom, the first Smith-vessel made a return trip to Earth, containing a delegation of Smithmen appointed to establish relations with the planet of their birth. They came not as visitors, but as representatives of another interplanetary power to the United Nations.

At first, the UN debated their sovereignty, and their right to deal with the Earth nations as a separate and distinct entity. There were days of arguments among the UN members, and a special commission was formed to study the question. Finally, they ruled that Smith's World was not a legally constituted entity, and therefore not entitled to recognition.

The delegation didn't seem surprised at the decision, and merely asked that the UN set up a trading commission between the planets, by which Earth could benefit from the fruits of the scientific progress made on Smith's World, in exchange for those materials which Earth could most readily provide. There were scientific demonstrations held in the now nearly deserted Smith Building in Flushing Meadows, demonstrations of electronic marvels that were unknown on Earth. An agreement of interplanetary trading rules was drawn up, and Smith's World was given its first unofficial recognition as a separate power.

It soon became apparent that the "material" most in demand on Smith's World was Manpower.

The testing began again, and lights, were burning brightly once more within the vast halls of the Smith Building. The Smith-standards were no longer so rigid, and of the four or five million candidates who volunteered in the year that followed, almost half a million were accepted for relocation on the new planet.

The Smith-rockets left every week, bringing a new cargo of human material to the tiny glowing pinpoint in the heavens.

To make the record clear, I want to state that the plot to kill Smith didn't originate with me. I no longer know whose scheme it was, which member of the Anti-Smith League was responsible for drafting the plan. One thing I'm sure of is that Alita herself wasn't the originator, although I heard the proposal from her lips first.

I met Alita by what I later realized was a staged incident. I was assigned by the magazine to cover a lecture that was being held in Town Hall by a Reverend Moore, a lecture provocatively titled: "Is Smith a God?" I accepted the job reluctantly, but my editor assumed that my past connection with Smith would be an asset in the preparation of such a story.

It wasn't the first time a religious leader had made public condemnation of Smith; pulpits all over the world had been ringing with phrases accusing Smith of usurping holy rights. But I suppose this event had greater significance, since the Reverend Harlow Moore had been Smith's own religious instructor in the bygone days of Smith's childhood.

Reverend Moore was a burly man with a humorous mouth and shaggy white hair in need of trimming. He did no pulpit pounding when he spoke of Smith. He spoke quietly to the Town Hall audience, a large crowd that filled every seat in the auditorium. He spoke at length about Smith, the child, describing his prowess as a Bible student, remarking upon his feat of learning Old and New Testaments word for word.

"I was impressed," he said with a twinkle. "Greatly impressed, having such a poor memory myself. But I must confess that I mistook this ability of Smith's. Our friend Smith didn't learn the Bible 'by heart'—only by mind. His heart was never involved, and his soul failed to grasp the deep meaning of the sacred writings. You have heard that the Devil can quote scriptures to his purpose; well, that means the Devil must have a good memory, too."

The lecture continued without heat or rancor, more of a plea for understanding than condemnation. When it was over, I pushed my way down the aisle of the hall. Somehow, in the crush to the exits, I found myself stepping hard on someone's toe, and a woman's voice cried out in pain.

"Gosh, I'm sorry—"

The face that turned towards me was of such striking beauty that I couldn't help staring. Her skin was creamy white, her eyes vividly sea-green, her mouth wide and sensuous. Her black hair was unusually long, and the total effect was of something pagan. She stumbled, and I put my arm out to help her through the crowds filling the aisle. Even through the fabric of her sleeve, her skin felt warm and good to the touch.

When we reached the street, she said: "They say liquor's good for snakebite. How about a crushed toe?"

"I don't know. We can try."

Five minutes later, we were in a cocktail lounge with a highball in front of her and a soft drink for me, learning each other's names and occupations, and discovering a mutual interest in Smith. Her name was Alita Morgan; she was a fashion designer and model. And her interest in Smith—

"Vincent and I were going to be married in the fall," she told me, her eyes downcast, her knuckles white around the glass. "Then he got interested in Smith's World, and wanted us to take the examinations together at Flushing Meadows. I refused, but Vince went on alone. He passed."

I said: "I'm sorry."

"Don't be. It was something that couldn't be helped. I'm glad I found out so soon. If Vince thought some manmade Heaven was more important than me—"

"And why didn't you go? Why didn't you take the examination?"

"Because," she answered coldly. "Because I'm too content with the God I have. I don't want any other, no matter how much Paradise he's selling."

"I guess that's how I feel," I said. "But who knows? Maybe we're both wrong. Maybe Smith doesn't demand that much of the people on his world."

She was studying my face.

"Luke Wingate," she said softly. "Now I remember. You were Smith's friend in college. You even worked for him some years ago."

"That's true."

"But you didn't go to Smith's World?"

"No. I like it here. I like it even better now."

She smiled. "Would you like to come to a party, Luke Wingate?"

The party was at Alita's Greenwich Village apartment, and there were no cocktails served, no jokes told, no hilarity at all. The atmosphere was grim and purposeful. The two dozen participants, the majority of them men, were obviously gathered by more serious motives than conviviality. They didn't call it that, but I realized that I was attending one of the earliest meetings of the Anti-Smith League.

One of the speakers of the group was a thin, scholarly man of middle years named Burgess. He was a professor of history at Columbia, and he told us:

"The future is already clear. Almost three-quarters of a million people have made the transference from Earth to Smith's World, and as the testing procedures go on, that figure will double and treble.

"But the mere number does not tell the whole story. It is the caliber of the people we are losing. Our best scientists in every field. Our trained engineers. Our most competent artists, writers, journalists, researchers. Many of our best business executives have been lured by the Smith-promises. And that's only the beginning.

"We must face the situation realistically. The attractions of Smith's World are so great that the drain on our most skilled and essential manpower is already becoming crucial. The crisis point looms—a crisis that may well result in a chaos that not even atomic war could bring."

"But what can we do?" Alita whispered.

"Fight," someone said. "Fight with every means at our command. Fight within the UN organization, fight within the sovereign nations, fight with legislature, with pressure, with sanctions. And if necessary—fight with great force."

I hadn't meant to say anything; I was only willing to be a spectator. But at these last words, I said:

"We would lose."

They looked at me.

"We would lose a battle by force. I know Smith. And you know yourself the accumulation of brainpower on Smith's World. Force is no answer, believe me."

"Whatever the answer," Burgess said, "we must try to find it."

There were hours more of sober conversation, and then the crowd departed. I stayed behind, and Alita and I shared some after-party coffee.

We sat at opposite ends of the sofa, talking quietly. It was the first time in over a year that I had been in such attractive feminine company, and the sight of her slim, long-legged figure beside me stirred my pulse.

She said: "I know how to fight Smith."

I moved closer to her.

"I'm tired of talking about Smith. There's been too much talk of Smith."

She didn't resist as my arms went around her.

"Let's forget Smith," I said. "Just for a little while. I'm more interested in you, Alita."

"All right," she said. "How many eggs do you like for breakfast?"

But in the middle of the night, Alita shifted and rose in the bed to light a cigarette. I muttered something, and she put the cigarette to my lips for a puff. Then she said:

"I know how to fight Smith."

"All right," I moaned. "How?"

"Kill him."

CHAPTER NINE

Alita held my arm tightly as we entered through the first doorway of the Smith-testing Division of the Smith Building. I patted her hand and said something meant to be reassuring.

The first clerk, wearing the gray Smith-uniform with the golden "S" on his sleeve, was cordial. He said:

"Your names, please?"

I cleared my throat.

"Mr. and Mrs. Lukas Wingate."

He walked to the computer and threw the activating switch. The machine chattered, and produced a narrow white punchcard. He came back with it, and handed it to us.

"Carry this with you at all times," he said. "You do understand the regulations concerning married couples? If either one of you fails to be accepted, the acceptable partner cannot gain permission to enter Smith's World without the consent of the other."

"We understand."

"Good. We wish to express to you our gratitude for your interest in Smith's World, and hope your examinations prove successful.

"Thank you," Alita said throatily, and we moved into the first testing zone.

I thought I knew what to expect the moment we got beyond the welcoming-stage of the Smith-testing, but I quickly discovered that the process of examination as I knew it during my employment had changed drastically. The physical tests were no more demanding than standard military service examinations. The mental tests were still strict, but the passing grade standard had been lowered to allow mentalities as average as my own to be passed. The psychological tests were simpler, too, but when the time came for me to face the inquisitor sitting behind the cold metal desk, I had my first doubts about my ability to attain my goal.

"Nice to see you, Mr. Wingate."

The psychiatrist was a dry-lipped, narrow man with brilliantly polished spectacles.

"You're rather a well known name around this organization," he said lightly, but without humor in his eyes. "Quite a lot has happened since you left Smith-employment."

"That's right," I said. "A lot happened."

"You were ill, I believe?"

"You can call it that. I was an alcoholic."

"I see. And how do you feel about liquor now?"

"It's all right for other people."

He nodded his head.

"And now you're married. That's quite a change in a man's life."

"Yes."

"Mrs. Wingate is a very attractive woman."

"Yes."

"How long have you two been married?"

"About four months."

"Uh-huh. And is everything—satisfactory?"

I frowned. "We were born for each other."

"I see. And if you don't mind the question, Mr. Wingate, what are your feelings about—" He looked down at the papers on his desk as if the name was written there. "About Evelyn Armour?"

"Who?"

"Come now, Mr. Wingate."

"Look, isn't this rather personal? Your boy Smith's invited me up there a dozen times. I'm no different now. Do we have to scrape around the past?"

"No, of course not," the psychiatrist said smoothly. "Then I gather that the old wound is—well, closed?"

"Absolutely. I love my wife and she loves me, and I'm dying to be Queen of the May. Now let's get this farce over with."

The psychiatrist smiled blandly.

"And what about Smith?"

"What about him?"

"How do you feel about Smith, Mr. Wingate? After all, it's no secret that Evelyn Armour was your fiancée before she joined Smith on our World. Do you harbor any resentment?"

"Naturally. As a matter of fact, the only reason I want to get to Smith's World is to punch him right in the nose."

The psychiatrist stiffened, and I saw that I had pushed my joke too far.

"Look, doc," I said, with a feeble grin. "I'm only kidding. Smith was one of my best friends, and I don't have any resentment left. We had some problems about Evelyn, but I'm over that now. Now I'm happily married, and everything's changed. Do you understand?"

"Perfectly." He took off his glasses and tried to shine even more brilliance into the lenses. "That's all, Mr. Wingate."

At the end of the testing line, my punchcard was handed back to me. I gave it to the final Smith-clerk, and he put it through a computer. When it emerged, he handed it back with a shrug of his shoulder.

Stamped across the card, in red ink, was one word.

"REJECTED."

"Sorry, Mr. Wingate," he said. "If you have any questions as to exactly why this decision was made, or if you wish to argue the case further, you may write to the Smith Appeals Board, at this address. If you're unsuccessful, perhaps you will want to take the Smith-tests again, after the official six-month lapse."

I met Alita outside.

Her card was stamped: "ACCEPTABLE."

"What do we do now?" I said glumly. "I suppose all that's left is for me to give my consent."

"No!" she said violently. "I won't leave without you, Luke."

"Hey, wait a minute." I pulled her towards me. "This was the deal, remember? It's strictly a business proposition. If both of us can't complete the assignment, then one of us must."

She began to cry, soundlessly.

"I can't go without you Luke. I don't care about the Anti-Smith League. I won't go anywhere without you."

"We'll talk about it," I said. "At home."

We were living at Alita's apartment in the Village, but before returning there, we stopped off at the apartment of Burgess, the history professor, to tell him the bad news.

When we finally reached home, there was a telegram beneath the door.

I t was addressed to me, and it read:

HAPPY TO INFORM YOU THAT SPECIAL DISPENSATION HAS BEEN MADE IN YOUR CASE. MRS. WINGATE AND YOURSELF MAY PREPARE TO LEAVE FOR SMITH'S WORLD ON NEXT SMITH FLIGHT JUNE 10.

DIRECTOR
SMITH TESTING DIV.

That was how Alita and I came to Smith's World.

We expected to find a world designed in Hollywood concepts, with sweeping skyscrapers and Disney landscapes, where the populace paraded about in clean white togas among green arbors, where the sun always shone and the birds sung sweetly, and everything was milk and honey and sweetness and light.

It was almost true, but not quite.

From the moment we debarked from the great Smith-rocket that brought us to Smith's World, we knew that Smith had designed a very practical planet. Much of its terrain was almost Spartan in its simplicity. Trees were planted only where shade was needed. Buildings were constructed for their functional requirements. Birds and animals were confined to restricted sanctuaries and woodland areas, and the game animals were severely bred and controlled for the purpose of providing food. There was just so much farmland, and just so much city area. There was no surface vehicle traffic whatsoever; the air was utilized for all transportation. There were no arbors for casual strolling and no togas anywhere in evidence. Both men and women wore modified Earth clothing, made distinctive only by subtleties of color. There was an air of industry about the streets of the city, but no sound of laughter. Uniformed Smith-officials were everywhere. I would say that nothing was more immediately apparent than those gray-suited Smith-officials with the golden "S" on their sleeves. None carried weapons, not overtly, and all were exceedingly polite and helpful. But there were so many of them—so many.

The rocket that delivered us to the new planet held over five hundred men and women. But it was clear that we were to be singled out for special attention. After the initial briefing and speech of welcome at the Smith Reception Center, the new Smith-dwellers were herded off into another section of the building for further orientation. But Alita and I were drawn aside by a smooth-faced Smith-official.

"Mr. and Mrs. Wingate?"

"Yes?"

"Would you be so kind as to follow me? You have been requested to share the evening meal with Smith."

Alita looked at me.

"That's fine," I said. "Be good to see the old boy."

The Smith-official's face did not alter.

At the copter station, waiting for the craft that would take us to the quarters of the planet's overlord, we had a moment to ourselves. Alita whispered to me: "So soon, Luke! To get the chance so soon!"

The thought chilled me, and I gripped her hand.

"Maybe we shouldn't. Maybe we should wait..."

"No. The sooner the better," Alita answered grimly. Then her dark expression was exchanged for a sunny smile as the Smith-official returned to our side.

CHAPTER TEN

We boarded a copter that lifted us above the streets of the capital city, and swayed in the direction of the tallest edifice to be seen on Smith's World—a white steeple of a building, crowned in glass. We were hovering above it in seconds, and the copter pilot was guiding the craft expertly to the landing platform that formed a balcony around the top of the needle-shaped structure.

Upon landing, another Smith-official took us in tow, this time openly carrying a weapon.

First, there was a corridor, stretching towards a white door. We were scanned photo-electrically. Alita passed the scrutiny, but the metal of my belt buckle set off a warning buzzer. The guard asked me to remove my belt, and I did. This time, the metal-seeking eyes were silent. Alita and I exchanged glances as we were told to go ahead, thinking the same thought. We were carrying a weapon, but not one that would respond to Smith's warning system. At that moment, I lost some respect for Smith, at his inability to know about the deadly device concealed in Alita's long black hair.

Then the doors opened, and we were in the Chambers.

I expected a throne room, but I was wrong. It was a room furnished in the manner of a super modern executive suite, with polished marble floors and an enormous crescent-shaped desk. And behind the desk, his dry-straw hair now streaked with gray, but otherwise unchanged: Smith.

I can't recall now what was said in those first few minutes of our reunion. They were all pleasant words, commonplace words about simple things, words ill-suited to the situation of a disbeliever reunited with a God. There was no handshake; there never was with Smith. But he was courteous; there was a smoothness in his manner I'd never known before. He was gallant towards Alita, and made a pretty speech to me about my good taste in women.

"You flatter me," Alita said. "I understand from Luke that you have good taste yourself."

Smith didn't react to the thinly-veiled mention of Evelyn. Instead, he smiled and gestured towards the curved dome of glass that surrounded his quarters.

"What do you think of my world, Luke?" he said. "Have I done things well?"

"Very well. It's not what I expected though—"

"There was no sense in being too radical, not at first. One of our most serious problems on Smith's World is—well, call it nostalgia, homesickness, what you will. So I designed my planet to give us the best of the old as well as the new. In time, there will be changes. I have many plans. I'm glad you've come to share them with me."

I looked at Alita, and saw her hand toying with her hair.

I gasped and said: "Wait!"

"What is it?" Smith said.

"Nothing." My pulse was almost audible. "I—I have a favor to ask, Smith. One small favor."

"Anything, Luke."

"I want to see Evelyn."

I could see the dismay in Alita's face, but I went on.

"For old time's sake, Smith. You can understand that."

"Surely," he said. "I anticipated that you would, Luke. "She's in the next room, right now." His eyes went to a doorway at the side of the room. "She's alone. Why not go in now?"

"All right." I looked at Alita. "Wait for me."

Her mouth was sullen, but I turned on my heel and went to the door. Before I touched it, it slid back to reveal a barren gray-walled room, with one chair. Rising to greet me was Evelyn. The door closed behind me.

What had I expected? What effect did I anticipate upon seeing Evelyn again? I didn't know myself.

She was lovelier than ever, but her loveliness seemed to have mellowed with time. There was no longer a star-brightness about her; she radiated a soft, golden light of a summer's moon. She was dressed simply, in white.

"Evelyn," I said.

"Hello, Luke. I'm so glad you came to our World."

"It's been a long time." I felt inane and foolish, my tongue thick and heavy.

"Yes, it has," Evelyn said.

"Are you—happy?"

"Very happy, Luke."

I frowned at the answer. I wanted to hurt her suddenly. I said: "I'm married now, you know."

"So I've heard. I'm glad for you, Luke. They tell me your bride is very beautiful."

I took a step towards her.

"Evelyn—"

She must have seen what was in my eyes, because she answered: "Don't, Luke. Don't touch me. I love Smith. I worship Smith."

"Worship?" My mouth jerked at the word.

"Yes, worship. He's a God, Luke. I know that now. He's truly a God."

"You don't know what you are saying. He's got you hypnotized. You're playing Trilby to his Svengali—"

"You're wrong, Luke. He is a God." Her eyes shone. "You thought you knew Smith, but you didn't, not really. Nobody knows him as I do. If you could see the things he can do. He can appear and disappear at will, Luke. He is everywhere, anywhere. He can work miracles, Luke!"

"Tricks!" I said angrily. "You've been taken in by his tricks, Evelyn. He's got some gadget that projects his image around the place. He used it on me, one night back on Earth. It's only a machine—"

She shook her head, and there was an indulgent smile on her face. "You're wrong. You don't know. You just don't know, Luke."

The door behind us slid open again.

"Was it a pleasant reunion?" Smith said, still standing behind the desk.

"Very pleasant," Evelyn smiled at him.

I walked back into the main chamber, trying to hide the emotion crossing my face. The door closed behind her, as if it were a vault closing upon some fragile jewel of great worth.

"Now," Smith said softly, "we can dine together."

"Yes," I said to Alita. "Now."

Her hand went to her hair, in a womanly gesture. But when her fingers emerged, they were holding a thin cylinder of bamboo. It was an ancient, primitive weapon, and strangely fitting to end the life of a super-scientist on his man-created world. She placed the cylinder to her lips, and a puff of her breath sent the poison-drenched splinter towards the figure behind the desk.

He continued to smile.

"I'm sorry, Smith," I said. "This had to be done."

Alita stared, waiting for his fall.

It didn't come.

Then Smith laughed.

"I apologize," he said. "There is no humor in this moment for you, I know that. But as for me, the spectacle is amusing. I must congratulate you on the simplicity of your attack. Other assassins have been far more clever in their techniques—and never got this far. But a blowgun and a poisoned dart—" He chuckled, but he didn't die.

"I don't understand," Alita gasped. "I didn't miss. I couldn't have—"

"No," Smith said. "You didn't miss, my dear."

Then I knew why our scheme had failed. We weren't looking at Smith at all; he hadn't trusted us to that extent. We were the guests of a spectral host; Smith's body was in another room of the citadel; our dart had whistled through a phantom image, electronically projected.

"I'm sorry to find you still an enemy," Smith said sadly. "I had hoped that things had changed between us, Luke. Now you leave me no other choice but to forget my debt to you."

Behind us, the white door was sliding open, and the Smith-officials were entering with drawn weapons.

It was a shock for me to realize that there was a prison on Smith's World; it was an admission of imperfection and discontent. It was even more of a shock when I discovered that the subterranean cells, located some eighty miles from Smith's citadel, numbered in the thousands—and were all occupied.

Alita and I were separated, and I was marched through long stone corridors from one dismal chamber to another. There was little modernity in evidence; it might have been the catacombs of any ancient prison on Earth. It was damp and poorly lighted, and the officials assigned to its ugly duties bore the same stamp of insensitive cruelty that marked jailers of every period in history. I was fingerprinted, photographed, and treated with callow disrespect. My head was shaved and my body deloused, and my first taste of the food in Smith-prison told me that my God-like friend had little interest in the wellbeing of those who broke his holy laws. My cell was cold; the walls wet; the cot sagging and springless; the light a naked bulb of meager wattage. It was more of a dungeon than a prison; a storage place for the human refuse of Smith's World.

But miserable as my life in Smith's prison was to be, it was there that I discovered Smith's weaknesses as a God. And it was in the Smith-prison that I learned that Smith's World had an Anti-Smith League, too.

I determined that fact slowly, on those few occasions when the Smith-prisoners were permitted an exchange of low-voiced conversation. An elderly man, with a dragging left leg and a palsied hand, borrowed a cigarette from me one day and said:

"The Earth looks red tonight."

"What's that?"

"My cell window faces west; I can see the Earth glowing at night. It glows redder and redder all the time. They say a day will come when the Earth will bleed, and Smith's World will burn."

I thought he was feebleminded, and began to move away. He put his arm on mine.

"No!" he said hoarsely. "You must listen carefully. You're new here." He peered at me more closely. "And your face is familiar. Did we meet back on Earth?"

I looked at him again. My throat tightened when I recognized Dr. Martin Corcoran, the brilliant biophysicist I had personally lured into Smith's service during my California trip. I grasped his trembling hand, and asked his forgiveness.

"Only Smith is to blame," he said. "Smith and all of us who mistook him for a God. But he is a man, and an imperfect one. I have been here many months, in this prison, and I have learned more within these walls than I could have in freedom on Smith's World. I will tell you what I have learned, Mr. Wingate. Perhaps the facts will be useful to you some day."

"What did you mean?" I said, "about the Earth turning red?"

He looked about him cautiously.

"There are almost three thousand prisoners here. But this is not a criminal prison. Do you see what that means?"

"No."

"These are not thieves and murderers. These are rebels, rebels against Smith. Three thousand out of a population of less than two million. Can you imagine the great number still not discovered and imprisoned?"

"A revolt?" I stared at him. "But how? Why?"

"Why is the simpler question. You must have lived on Smith's World to know. You must have learned about your duties on this planet; duties only to Smith, never to yourself, to your children, to your friends, to humanity. There are no churches on Smith's World; each building is a temple designed for the worship of Smith. Do you know how much of your mind, and your body, and your soul Smith demands? All of it, my friend."

"But how can you fight him? It's *his* world—"

"Perhaps. But many of us have decided to fight. To fight or to die. That is enough."

"And when will it happen?"

Corcoran shrugged wearily.

"Younger bodies than mine must fix the date."

A Smith-guard approached us, and the old man fell silent.

CHAPTER ELEVEN

As the weeks dragged on, I spent as much time as I could in Corcoran's company, listening to him tell of life on Smith's World: a world without end; a world where Nature was subservient to Man, and Man subservient to Smith...

Then I met the others. Scientists, researchers, writers, engineers, artists, philosophers. There were two of the historians I myself had hired for Smith's World. There were four rocket-pilots among the prisoners, and what I learned from them was startling and deeply disturbing. I met them and I listened to them, and the more I heard, the more I wanted to dig my way out of the Smith-prison, with my bare fingernails, if no other escape could be found.

One day, I spoke to Corcoran about escape.

He shook his head. "No, Luke. Smith has been careful. He has executed no prisoners, fearing repercussions from Earth. He is not yet strong enough to ignore Earth's enmity. But he has made certain that no escape is possible. The prison is ringed by a series of radioactive screens. Guards and prisoners arrive and depart by a single copter on the roof, and that is protected night and day, by a stringent security system. The precautions are great; no successful escape has been made."

"Then it's hopeless?"

"From within, yes. But I see the Earth from my window, and each day, it grows redder and redder."

Then he turned and shuffled away.

I had been in Smith's prison for eight months, when Evelyn came into my cell.

I thank God for the strength of the vessels that bring blood into my heart, for if there had been weakness there, it would have destroyed me that night. When I heard the whispering sound within the cell, and stirred to see what caused it, the sight of Evelyn shocked me so greatly that I literally reeled and almost fainted.

But I recovered, and saw Evelyn, lovelier than ever, dressed coolly in white, her long blonde hair flowing behind her like a golden cloud.

"Luke," she whispered, tears glistening on her cheeks. "Luke, it's Evelyn. I must talk to you."

I couldn't speak.

"Don't be frightened. It's Smith's machine, his electronic projection device. I'm at Smith's citadel. Smith isn't here; there's some kind of trouble in the farmlands; he had to go there."

"Evelyn!" I gasped finally. "For the love of God, are you crazy?"

"Luke, listen to me. I have to explain something. I—I was troubled about what you told me, about Smith's ability to appear and disappear. I asked him point-blank after your arrest. He laughed and admitted it. He showed me the machine, taught me how to operate it—"

"Then you know he's not a God. Do you know that, Evelyn?"

She hid her face in her hands.

"I don't know anything, Luke! I'm so confused—"

I put my arm out towards her, my fingers aching to touch her. But I knew there was only air in the lovely body at the foot of my prison cot.

Then she straightened up and said: "Luke, I want to help you. He's talking wildly about you. He says you're the most dangerous man on his world. I don't know why he thinks that, but he does. He's fighting with himself over you, Luke. Part of him wants to save you, the other part wants to kill you. But he's beginning to change, Luke. All this trouble is changing him—"

"What trouble?"

"I don't understand it exactly. There have been strikes, riots, outbreaks. I don't know why; I don't see why people aren't happy. He's given them everything, Luke. Why should they not be happy?"

I sneered, but said nothing.

"There's some awful movement underway, Luke. There's been talk about a Bleeding Earth. I don't know what they mean by it, but it frightens me. There—there was another assassination attempt last week. It failed, of course. They always fail. But I'm so worried, Luke—"

She began to sob.

"Get hold of yourself," I said. "Did you mean that about wanting to help me?"

"Yes!"

"Then you can get me out of here, Evelyn. You can get me out right now. Do the prison officials know you?"

"Yes."

"Then you can have me released. Make it a command, Evelyn; they'll listen to you."

She gasped. "They won't! Only Smith can order a release."

"Tell them your orders come from Smith. They're so frightened of him that they'll listen, Evelyn. Appear before the prison warden. He'll be afraid to disobey you, Evelyn; afraid of anyone so close to Smith as you are—"

She turned away.

"All right," she said at last. "I'll try, Luke."

That was how I made my escape from Smith-prison, the only man to accomplish the feat.

I had been gambling with the fears of the Smith-officials in telling Evelyn to speak for Smith, and the gamble had won. Within an hour after her visit to my cell, a trio of Smith-guards came and unlocked my door. They guided me to the roof of the prison, and a copter took me back to the relative freedom of Smith's needle-shaped citadel.

I found Evelyn waiting for me in Smith's chamber. But the moment I saw her, I made a mistake. I asked:

"What have they done with Alita?"

Her moist eyes became dry and hard.

"I don't know. What does it matter, Luke? You don't love that woman. You married her as part of the scheme to assassinate Smith. That's the truth, isn't it?"

I didn't answer. I rubbed my heavy-whiskered cheeks and said: "I'd like to shave."

"In there."

In Smith's enormous bathroom, I took my first shower in eight months, and felt the good sensation of a sharp razor against my cheeks. I dressed myself out of Smith's private wardrobe, and came back to the Smith-chamber.

Evelyn was at the dome, looking at the glowing ball over our heads, the planet of our birth.

"It's so red tonight..."

"Red?"

I pushed her aside and looked out at the horizon of Smith's World. The sky was red, the clouds red, and even the speck in the sky appeared reddened by some mysterious distant fire.

"It is red," I said. "There are flames somewhere, flames to the east..."

"The farmland!" she whispered.

"They're burning the fields! Is that the trouble you meant?"

"I don't know!" She clutched at her throat. "Smith didn't tell me anything. He just said—trouble."

"It's started," I muttered. "The Earth is bleeding."

"Oh, Luke, I'm frightened!"

She was in my arms, soft and warm and yielding.

Neither of us heard the door sliding open behind us.

"Well," Smith said. "What's fair is fair, eh, Luke? Isn't that what the old Bible said? But of course. 'An eye for an eye'…"

I turned to face him, holding Evelyn behind me.

"Your world is burning, Smith."

He laughed. "So I understand. Nero's world burned, too, as I recall. But he managed all right."

Smith looked very fatigued. When he came towards us, his steps were faltering. Evelyn moaned at his approach, but he passed us by and went to the glass.

"What is it?" I said. "The Bleeding Earth?"

He smiled at me, wryly.

"Then you know of my little rebellious movement? Yes, the Bleeding Earth. A pretty name for the renegades. Almost Biblical." He put his head against the cool glass. *"'And when the people saw that Moses delayed to come down out of the mount, the people gathered themselves together unto Aaron, and said unto him, Up, make us gods, which shall go before us; for as for this Moses, the man that brought us up out of Egypt, we wot not what is become of him.'…"*

Evelyn whimpered, and cowered against me.

"'…and Moses' anger waxed hot,'" Smith said. *"'and he cast the tablets out of his hands, and break them beneath the mount.'…"*

Smith laughed, and turned to me.

"Now you see my mistake, Luke. Not to have continued with my evolution experiments. To have relied upon this sorry breed to people my new world…"

"Your world, Smith?"

He looked at me sharply. I pushed Evelyn aside and stepped towards him.

"Is it truly your world, Smith? Created by your marvelous world-building machine? Is that how it came into being?"

He said nothing.

"Or is it really God's world, Smith? Did you find that your fine machine didn't really work in the limits of space? That you weren't nearly so capable of creating planets as you thought?"

"What are you saying, Luke?" His voice was still unruffled.

"I know the truth, Smith. You never created Smith's World out of the dust of the cosmos. This was a God-created planet, Smith. Your ships captured and steered it into the orbital paths of this solar system; you didn't 'create' it at all. Am I speaking the truth?"

From the window, the sky blazed redder, and the crimson cast fell across Smith's face.

"You're a great scientist, Smith. No one denies you that. But you're not a God. Not nearly a God. You can make marvels, yes, but small marvels compared to the wonders of God. You can't make miracles, Smith. It's only a pose— pose of your insane ego. You're crazy, Smith!" I was shouting now. "You're crazy!"

I never reckoned what effect my words would have on him. At first, all his reaction was in his eyes. They burned out at me with such terrible rage that I was forced to look away. Then his hands started to jerk, his fingers moving convulsively, until he had to clench them into fists to stop their involuntary motions. Then he raised his arms above his head and began to speak. The words were unintelligible; but they were Holy Writ; I could tell that from their sonorous, rhythmical cadence; but his voice had lost all power to distinguish between vowels and consonants, words and animal sounds.

Then he lowered his arms, slowly, and spoke quietly to us, almost conversationally.

"It's all very well," he said. "This little rebellion of theirs. They think they're fighting for their freedom, but they're wrong. It's not freedom they'll win, Luke. Only death."

"What are you talking about?"

"The citadel. This building. They'll be coming here, finally. That's the logical thing for them to do. They'll storm it as the French stormed the Bastille, crying words of liberty and equality." He made a noise in his throat, and it was ugly. "But they'll be surprised, Luke. Terribly surprised at what happens."

"What about the building?"

"Why, it's not a building at all. Not really. These are the only chambers, you see. Just these rooms, for Evelyn and myself. The rest of the structure is really a stockpile, Luke. An atomic stockpile; the final precaution you might say."

I went cold down to my feet; the very floor beneath me held a threat.

"You're lying," I said.

"I'm telling you the truth, Luke. If my rebels come here, they destroy Smith's World and themselves." He chuckled. "It was one of my best ideas, Luke. Don't you agree?"

CHAPTER TWELVE

I wheeled towards the window. The fire was angrier in the night sky, and my ears picked out the sound of voices below.

"We'll have to get out of here," I said. "Evelyn—"

She was looking at Smith, but she said to me: "There's a copter on the roof—"

"Then let's go—"

I grabbed her arm, but she jerked away from me. Her eyes were still fixed on Smith, and the God of Smith's World was going to his knees.

This time, his words were audible.

"My God, my God, why hast Thou forsaken me? Why art Thou so far from helping me, and from the words of my roaring? O, my God, I cry in the daytime but Thou hearest not; and in the night season, and am not silent..."

"Smith!" Evelyn shrieked.

"Look at his eyes," I said. "He can't hear you now—"

"We must go, Evelyn—"

"I can't! I can't leave him."

"You'll have to leave him. If the mob reaches the citadel—"

"But he *needs* me, Luke!"

Now I heard the shouts clearly in the street far below. I tried again to make Evelyn come with me, but her arms were steel-strong around the stooped body of Smith.

I left her, and went to the roof.

There were people running everywhere in the streets when I brought the copter to ground. Some tried to climb aboard, shouting:

"To the spaceport! Please take me! The spaceships are leaving! I want to go home!"

The spaceships! The words struck me with their message of hope. If I could find Alita and reach the Smith-rockets before the mobs attacked...

Then I realized how hopeless it was. Alita was a prisoner in some unknown quarter of Smith's World, and only minutes were delaying the eruption of Smith's planet into atomic dust.

My mind rocked with the decision I had to make. To leave Alita behind, and take my chance of getting to safety— or to search the unknown streets and terrain until the moment when the pile was triggered, and all problems ended.

It was then I realized that my love for Alita was no manufactured thing. I loved her for what she was, and I knew that I would never see her again.

I guided the copter back into the sky, and followed the running crowds to the spaceport of Smith's World, and heard the rockets already beginning to explode, promising return to the planet of our birth and our true God.

These are my Smith-facts.

As you know by now, some sixty Smith-rockets left the planet before the atomic explosion that turned Smith's World into a black cinder. And you know that Alita was a passenger aboard one of those ships, one of three hundred women prisoners released by the rebels. Even now, I cannot speak of our reunion on Earth without clouded eyes.

We have a son, Alita and I.

He believes in God. We do, too.

THE END

HIGH INTRIGUE IN AN ALTERNATE UNIVERSE

For Brion Bayard, the discovery of an alternate world to Earth, where history took a different turn in the road, was not a pleasant experience. When he was kidnapped kicking and screaming, it brought him some startling revelations. Here was a world in which there were identical double personages—including a dangerous and most hated dictator named…Brion Bayard!

His assignment seemed simple enough. Dressed as the dictator's double, Brion was to enter the enemy stronghold, kill the dictator, and take his place until law and order could be maintained. Unfortunately, assassination attempts are a mighty tricky deal and things do not always go as planned…

CAST OF CHARACTERS

BRION BAYARD
This American diplomat had been kidnapped and specifically recruited to commit murder. The intended target…himself!

CHIEF INSPECTOR BALE
A detestable man, full of greed. He was feared and loathed—and it didn't matter which world he was on.

HERMANN GOERING
The same name, the same body, yet not the same man. There's no telling what you'll find in an alternate universe.

MANFRED VON RICHTHOFEN
The dreaded Bloody Red Baron? What was he doing here and what part would he play—honored hero or scathing cad?

BARBRO LUNDANE
There was a sweetish air to this Swedish lass, but was she really a good enough reason to leave one world for another?

GASTON
He didn't know why his brother wanted Bayard kept alive, but he was going to do his damnedest to honor the request.

BRION BAYARD (number two)
Who was this monster really? The merciless heathen he'd been made out to be, or a duped Dictator being played for a fool?

WORLDS OF THE
THE
IMPERIUM

By
KEITH LAUMER

ARMCHAIR FICTION
PO Box 4369, Medford, Oregon 97504

*For more information about Armchair Books and products, visit our
website at…*

www.armchairfiction.com

Or email us at…

armchairfiction@yahoo.com

CHAPTER ONE

I STOPPED in front of a shop with a small wooden sign, which hung from a wrought-iron spear projecting from the weathered stone wall. On it the word Antikvariat was lettered in spidery gold against dull black. The sign creaked as it swung in the night wind. Below it a metal grating covered a dusty window with a display of yellowed etchings, woodcuts, and lithographs, and a faded mezzotint. Some of the buildings in the pictures looked familiar, but here they stood in open fields, or perched on hills overlooking a harbor crowded with sails. The ladies in the pictures wore great bell-like skirts and bonnets with ribbons, and carried tiny parasols, while dainty-footed horses pranced before carriages in the background.

It wasn't the prints that interested me though, or even the heavy gilt frame embracing a tarnished mirror at one side; it was the man whose reflection I studied in the yellowed glass, a dark man wearing a tightly-belted grey trench coat that was six inches too long. He stood with his hands thrust deep in his pockets and stared into a darkened window fifty feet from me.

He had been following me all day.

At first I thought it was coincidence when I noticed the man on the bus from Bromma, then studying theatre announcements in the hotel lobby while I registered, and half an hour later sitting three tables away sipping coffee while I ate a hearty dinner.

I had discarded the coincidence theory a long time ago. Five hours had passed and he was still with me as I walked through the Old Town, medieval Stockholm still preserved on an island in the middle of the city. I had walked past shabby windows crammed with copper pots, ornate silver, dueling pistols, and worn cavalry sabres; they were all very quaint in the afternoon sun, but grim reminders of a ruder day of violence after midnight. Over the echo of my footsteps in the silent narrow streets the other steps came quietly behind, hurrying when I hurried, stopping when I stopped. Now the man stared into the dark window and waited. The next move was up to me.

I was lost. Twenty years is a long time to remember the tortuous turnings of the streets of the Old Town. I took my guidebook from my pocket and turned to the map in the back. My fingers were clumsy.

I craned my neck up at the stone tablet set in the corner of the building; it was barely legible: Master Samuelsgatan. I found the name on the folding map and saw that it ran for three short blocks, ending at Gamla Storgatan; a dead end. In the dim light it was difficult to see the fine detail on the map. I twisted the book around and got a clearer view; there appeared to be another tiny street, marked with cross-lines, and labeled Guldsmedstrappan.

I tried to remember my Swedish; *trappan* meant stair.

The Goldsmith's Stairs, running from Master Samuelsgatan to Hundgatan, another tiny street. It seemed to lead to the lighted area near the palace; it looked like my only route out. I dropped the book back into my pocket and moved off casually toward the stairs of the Goldsmith. I hoped there was no gate across the entrance.

My shadow waited a moment, then followed. As I was ambling, I slowly gained a little on him. He seemed in no hurry at all. I passed more tiny shops, with ironbound doors and worn stone sills, and then saw that the next doorway was an open arch with littered granite steps ascending abruptly. I paused idly, then turned in. Once past the portal, I bounded up the steps at top speed. Six leaps, eight, and I was at the top, darting to the left toward a deep doorway. There was just a chance I'd cleared the top of the stair before the dark man had reached the bottom. I stood and listened. I heard the scrape of shoes, then heavy breathing from the direction of the stairs a few feet away. I waited, breathing with my mouth wide open, trying not to pant audibly. After a moment the steps moved away. The proper move for my silent companion would be to cast about quickly for my hiding place, on the assumption that I had concealed myself close by. He would be back this way soon.

I risked a glance. He was moving quickly along, looking sharply about, with his back to me. I pulled off my shoes and without taking time to think about it, stepped out. I made it to the stairs in three paces, and faded out of sight as the man stopped to turn back. I leaped down three steps at a time; I was halfway down when my foot hit a loose stone, and I flew the rest of the way.

I hit the cobblestones shoulder first, and followed up with my head. I rolled over and scrambled to my feet, my head ringing. I clung to the wall by the foot of the steps as the pain started. Now I was getting mad. I heard the soft-shod feet coming down the stairs, and gathered myself to jump him as he came out. The footsteps hesitated just before the arch, then the dark round head with the uncut hair peeped out. I swung a haymaker—and missed.

He darted into the street and turned, fumbling in his overcoat. I assumed he was trying to get a gun, and aimed a kick at his mid-section. I had better luck this time; I connected solidly, and had the satisfaction of hearing him gasp in agony. I hoped he hurt as badly as I did. Whatever he was fumbling for came free then, and he backed away, holding the thing in his mouth.

"One-oh-nine, where in bloody blazes are you?" he said in a harsh voice, glaring at me. He had an odd accent. I realized the thing was some sort of microphone. "Come in, one-oh-nine, this job's going to pieces..." He backed away, talking, eyes on me. I leaned against the wall; I was hurt too badly to be very aggressive. There was no one else in sight. His soft shoes made whispering sounds on the paving stones. Mine lay in the middle of the street where I had dropped them when I fell.

Then there was a sound behind me. I whirled, and saw the narrow street almost blocked by a huge van. I let my breath out with a sigh of relief. Here was help.

Two men jumped down from the van, and without hesitation stepped up to me, took my arms and escorted me toward the rear of the van. They wore tight white uniforms, and said nothing.

"I'm all right," I said. "Grab that man." About that time I realized he was following along, talking excitedly to the men in white, and that the grip on my arms was more of a restraint than a support. I dug in my heels and tried to pull away. I remembered suddenly that the Stockholm police don't wear white uniforms.

I might as well not have bothered. One of them unclipped a thing like a tiny aerosol bomb from his belt and sprayed it into my face. I felt myself go limp.

CHAPTER TWO

THERE was a scratching sound which irritated me. I tried unsuccessfully to weave it into a couple of dreams before my subconscious gave up. I was lying on my back, eyes closed. I couldn't think where I was. I remembered a frightening dream about being followed, and then as I became aware of pain in my shoulder and head, my eyes snapped open. I was lying on a cot at the side of a small office; the scratching came from the desk where a dapper man in a white uniform sat writing. There was a humming sound and a feeling of motion.

I sat up. At once the man behind the desk looked up, rose, and walked over to me. He drew up a chair and sat down.

"Please don't be alarmed," he said in a clipped British accent. "I'm Chief Captain Winter. You need merely to assist in giving me some routine information, after which you will be assigned comfortable quarters." He said all this in a smooth lifeless way, as though he'd been through it before. Then he looked directly at me for the first time.

"I must apologize for the callousness with which you were handled; it was not my intention. However," his tone changed, "you must excuse the operative; he was uninformed."

Chief Captain Winter opened a notebook and lolled back in his chair with pencil poised. "Where were you born, Mr. Bayard?"

They must have been through my pockets, I thought; they know my name.

"Who the hell are you?" I said.

The chief captain raised an eyebrow. His uniform was immaculate, and brilliantly jeweled decorations sparkled on his chest.

"Of course you are confused at this moment, Mr. Bayard, but everything will be explained to you carefully in due course. I am an Imperial officer, duly authorized to interrogate subjects under detention." He smiled soothingly. "Now please state your birthplace."

I said nothing. I didn't feel like answering any questions; I had too many of my own to ask first. I couldn't place the fellow's accent. He was an Englishman all right, but I couldn't have said from what part of England. I glanced at the medals. Most of them were strange but I recognized the scarlet ribbon of the Victoria Cross, with three palms, ornamented with gems. There was something extremely phony about Chief Captain Winter.

"Come along now, old chap," Winter said sharply. "Kindly co-operate. It will save a great deal of unpleasantness."

I looked at him grimly. "I find being chased, grabbed, gassed, stuffed in a cell, and quizzed about my personal life pretty damned unpleasant already, so don't bother trying to keep it all on a high plane. I'm not answering any questions." I reached in my pocket for my passport; it wasn't there.

"Since you've already stolen my passport, you know by now that I'm an American diplomat, and enjoy diplomatic immunity to any form of arrest, detention, interrogation and what have you. So I'm leaving as soon as you return my property, including my shoes."

Winter's face had stiffened up. I could see my act hadn't had much impression on him. He signaled, and two fellows I hadn't seen before moved around into view. They were bigger than he was.

"Mr. Bayard, you must answer my questions, under duress, if necessary. Kindly begin by stating your birthplace."

"You'll find it in my passport," I said. I was looking at the two reinforcements; they were as easy to ignore as a couple of bulldozers in the living room. I decided on a change of tactics. I'd play along in the hope they'd relax a bit, and then make a break for it.

One of the men, at a signal, handed Winter my passport from his desk. He glanced through it, made a number of notes, and passed the booklet back to me.

"Thank you, Mr. Bayard," he said pleasantly. "Now let's get on to particulars. Where did you attend school?"

I tried hard now to give the impression of one eager to please. I regretted my earlier truculence; it made my present pose of cooperativeness a little less plausible. Winter must have been accustomed to the job though, and to subjects who were abject. After a few minutes he waved an arm at the two bouncers, who left the room silently.

Winter had gotten on to the subject of international relations and geopolitics now, and seemed to be fascinated by my commonplace replies. I attempted once or twice to ask why it was necessary to quiz me closely on matters of general information, but was firmly guided back to the answering of the questions.

He covered geography and recent history thoroughly with emphasis on the period 1879-1910, and then started in on a biographic list; all I knew about one name after another. Most of them I'd never heard of, a few were minor public figures. He quizzed me in detail on two Italians, Cocino and Maxoni. He could hardly believe I'd never heard of them. He seemed fascinated by many of my replies.

"Niven an actor?" he said incredulously. "Never heard of Crane Talbot?" and when I described Churchill's role in recent affairs, he laughed uproariously.

After forty minutes of this one-sided discussion, a buzzer sounded faintly, and another uniformed man entered, placed a good-sized box on the corner of the desk, and left. Winter ignored the interruption.

Another twenty minutes of questions went by. Who was the present monarch of Anglo-Germany? Winter asked. What was the composition of the royal family, the ages of the children? I exhausted my knowledge of the subject. What was the status of the Viceroyalty of India? Explain the working of the Dominion arrangements of Australia, Northern America, Cabotsland...? I was appalled at the questions; the author of them must have been insane. It was almost impossible to link the garbled reference to non-existent political subdivisions and institutions to reality. I answered as matter-of-factly as possible. At least Winter did not seem to be much disturbed by my revision of his distorted version of affairs.

At last Winter rose, moved over to his desk, and motioned me to a chair beside it. As I pulled the chair out, I glanced into the box on the desk. I saw magazines, folded cloth, coins—and the butt of a small automatic protruding from under a copy of the World Almanac. Winter had turned away, reaching into a small cabinet behind the desk. My hand darted out, scooped up the pistol, and dropped it into my pocket as I seated myself.

Winter turned back with a blue glass bottle. "Now let's have a drop and I'll attempt to clear up some of your justifiable confusion, Mr. Bayard," he said genially. "What would you like to know?" I ignored the bottle.

"Where am I?" I said.

"In the city of Stockholm, Sweden."

"We seem to be moving; what is this, a moving van with an office in it?"

"This is a vehicle, though not a moving van."

"Why did you pick me up?"

"I'm sorry that I can tell you no more than that you were brought in under specific orders from a very high-ranking officer of the Imperial Service." He looked at me speculatively. "This was most unusual," he added.

"I take it kidnapping inoffensive persons is not in itself unusual."

Winter frowned. "You are the subject of an official operation of Imperial Intelligence. Please rest assured you are not being persecuted."

"What is Imperial Intelligence?"

"Mr. Bayard," Winters said earnestly, leaning forward, "it will be necessary for you to face a number of realizations; the first is that the governments which you are accustomed to regard as supreme sovereign powers must in fact be considered tributary to the Imperium, the Paramount Government in whose service I am an officer."

"You're a fake," I said.

Winter bristled. "I hold an Imperial Commission as Chief Captain of Intelligence."

"What do you call this vehicle we're in?"

"This is an armed TNL scout based at Stockholm Zero Zero."

"That tells me a lot; what is it, a boat, car, airplane...?"

"None of those, Mr. Bayard."

"All right, I'll be specific; what does it travel on, water, air...?

Winter hesitated. "Frankly, I don't know."

I saw it was time to try a new angle of attack. "Where are we going?"

"We are presently operating along coordinates zero-zero-zero, zero-zero-six, zero-ninety-two."

"What is our destination? What place?"

"Stockholm Zero Zero, after which you'll probably be transferred to London Zero Zero for further processing."

"What is the Zero business? Do you mean London, England?"

"The London you refer to is London B-I Three."

"What's the difference?"

"London Zero Zero is the capital of the Imperium, comprising the major portion of the civilized world—North Europe, West Hemisphere, and Australia."

I changed the subject. "Why did you kidnap me?"

"A routine interrogational arrest, insofar as I know."

"Do you intend to release me?"

"Yes."

"At home?"

"No."

"Where?"

"I can't say; at one of several concentration points."

"One more question," I said, easing the automatic from my pocket and pointing it at the third medal from the left. "Do you know what this is?"

"Keep your hands in sight; better get up and stand over there."

Winter rose and moved over to the spot indicated. I'd never aimed a pistol at a man point-blank before, but I felt no hesitation now.

"Tell me all about it," I said.

"I've answered every question," Winter said nervously.

"And told me nothing." Winter stood staring at me.

I slipped the safety off with a click. "You have five seconds to start," I said. One...two..."

"Very well," Winter said. "No need for all this; I'll try." He hesitated. "You were selected from higher up. We went to a great deal of trouble to get you in particular. As I've explained, that's rather irregular. However," Winter seemed to be warming to his subject, "all sampling in this region has been extremely restricted in the past; you see, your continuum occupies an island, one of a very few isolated lines in a vast blighted region. The entire configuration is abnormal, and an extremely dangerous area in which to maneuver. We lost many good men in early years before we learned how to handle the problems involved."

"I suppose you know this is all nonsense to me," I said. "What do you mean by sampling?"

"Do you mind if I smoke?" Winter asked. I took a long brown cigarette from a box on the desk, lit it, and handed it to him. "Sampling refers to the collection of individuals or artifacts from representative B-I lines," he said, blowing out smoke. "We in Intelligence are engaged now in mapping operations. It's fascinating work, old boy, picking up the trend lines, coordinating findings with theoretical work, developing accurate calibrating devices, instruments, and so on. We're just beginning to discover the potentialities of working the Net. In order to gather maximum information in a short time, we've found it expedient to collect individuals for interrogation. In this way we quickly gain a general picture of the configuration of the Net in various directions. In your case, I was directed under sealed orders to enter the Blight, proceed to Blight-Insular Three, and take over custody of Mr. Brion Bayard, a diplomat representing, of all things, an American republic." Winter spoke enthusiastically now. As he relaxed, he seemed younger.

"It was quite a feather in my cap, old chap, to be selected to conduct an operation in the Blight, and I've found it fascinating. Always in the past, of course, I've operated at such a distance from the Imperium that little or no analogy existed. But B-I Three! Why it's practically the Imperium, with just enough variation to stir the imagination. Close as the two lines are, there's a desert of Blight around and between them that indicates how frightfully close to the rim we've trodden in times past."

"All right, Winter. I've heard enough," I said. "You're just a harmless nut, maybe. But I'll be going now."

"That's quite impossible," Winter said. "We're in the midst of the Blight."

"What's the Blight?" I asked, making conversation as I looked around the room, trying to pick out the best door to leave by. There were three. I decided on the one no one had come through yet. I moved towards it.

"The Blight is a region of utter desolation, radiation, and chaos," Winter was saying. "There are whole ranges of A-lines where the very planet no longer exists, where automatic cameras have recorded nothing but a vast ring of debris in orbit; then there are the cinder-worlds, and here and there dismal groups of cancerous jungles, alive with radiation-poisoned mutations. It's frightful, old chap. You can wave the pistol at me all night, but it will get you nothing. In a few hours we'll arrive at Zero Zero; you may as well relax until then."

I tried the door, it was locked. "Where's the key?" I said.

"There's no key. It will open automatically at the base." I went to one of the other doors, the one the man with the box had entered through. I pulled it open and glanced out. The humming sound was louder and down a short and narrow corridor I saw what appeared to be a pilot's compartment. A man's back was visible.

"Come on, Winter," I said. "Go ahead of me."

"Don't be a complete ass, old boy," Winter said, looking irritated. He turned toward his desk. I raised the pistol. The shot boomed inside the walls of the room, and Winter leaped back from the desk holding a ripped hand. He whirled on me, for the first time looking really scared. "You're insane," he shouted. "I've told you we're in the midst of the Blight."

I was keeping one eye on the man up front, who was looking over his shoulder while frantically doing something with his other hand.

"You're leaking all over that nice rug," I said. "I'm going to kill you with the next one. Stop this machine."

Winter was pale; he swallowed convulsively. "I swear, Mr. Bayard, that's utterly impossible. I'd rather you shoot me. You have no conception of what you're suggesting."

I saw now that I was in the hands of a dangerous lunatic. I believed Winter when he said he'd rather die than stop this bus—or whatever it was. In spite of my threat, I couldn't shoot him in cold blood. I turned and took three steps up the passage and poked the automatic into the small of the back that showed there.

"Cut the switch," I said. The man, who was one of the two who had been standing by when I awoke in the office, continued to twist frantically at a knob on the panel before him. He glanced at me, but kept on twiddling. I raised the pistol and fired a shot into the instrument panel. The man jumped convulsively, and threw himself forward, protecting the panel with his body.

"Stop, you bloody fool," he shouted. "Let us explain!"

"I tried that," I said. "It didn't work. Get out of my way. I'm bringing this wagon to a halt one way or another."

I stood so that I could see both men. Winter half crouched in the doorway, face white. "Are we all right, Doyle?" he called in a strained voice. Doyle eased away from the panel, turned his back to me, and glanced over the instruments. He flipped a toggle, cursed, and turned back to face Winter.

"Communicator dead," he said. "But we're still in operation."

I hesitated now. These two were genuinely terrified of the idea of stopping; they had paid as little attention to me and my noisy gun as one would to a kid with a water pistol. Compared to stopping, a bullet was apparently a trifling irritation.

It was also obvious that this was no moving van. The pilot's compartment had more instruments than an airliner, and no windows. Elaborate ideas began to run through my mind. Space ship? Time machine? What the devil had I gotten into?

"All right, Winter," I said. "Let's call a truce. I'll give you five minutes to give me a satisfactory explanation, prove you're not an escapee from the violent ward, and tell me how you're going to go about setting me down right back where you found me. If you can't or won't cooperate, I'll fill that panel full of holes—including anybody who happens to be standing in front of it."

"Yes," Winter said. "I swear I'll do all I can. Just come away from the control compartment."

"I'll stay right here," I said. "I won't jump the gun unless you give me a reason, like holding your mouth wrong."

Winter was sweating. "This is a scouting machine, operating in the Net. By the Net, I mean the complex of Alternative lines, which constitute the matrix of all simultaneous reality. Our drive is the Maxoni-Cocini field generator, which creates a force operating at what one might call a perpendicular to normal entropy. Actually, I know little about the physics of the mechanism; I am not a technician."

I looked at my watch. Winter got the idea. "The Imperium is the government of the Zero Zero A-line in which this discovery was made. The device is an extremely complex one, and there are a thousand ways in which it can cause disaster to its operators if a mistake is made. Judging from the fact that every A-line within thousands of parameters of Zero Zero is a scene of the most fearful carnage, we surmise that our line alone was successful in controlling the force. We conduct our operations in all of that column of A-space lying outside the Blight, as we term this area of destruction. The Blight itself we ordinarily avoid completely."

Winter wrapped a handkerchief around his bleeding hand as he talked.

"Your line, known as Blight-Insular Three, or B-I Three, is one of two exceptions we know to the general destruction. These two lines lie at some distance from Zero Zero, yours a bit closer than B-I Two. B-I Three was discovered only a month or so ago, and just recently confirmed as a safe line. All this exploratory work in the Blight was done by drone scouts, unmanned.

"Why I was directed to pick you up, I don't know. But believe me when I say that if you succeed in crippling this scout, you'll precipitate us into identity with an A-line which might be nothing more than a ring of radioactive dust around the sun, or a great mass of mutated fungus. We cannot stop now for any reason until we reach a safe area."

I looked at my watch again. "Four minutes," I said. "Prove what you've been telling me."

Winter licked his lips. "Doyle, get the recon photos of this sector, the ones we made on the way in."

Doyle reached across to a compartment under the panel and brought out a large red envelope. He handed it to me. I passed it to Winter.

"Open it," I said. "Let's see what you've got."

Winter fumbled a moment, then slipped a stack of glossy prints out. He handed me the first one. "All these photos were made from precisely the same spatial and temporal coordinates as those occupied by the scout. The only difference is the Web coordinates."

The print showed an array of ragged fragments of rock hanging against a backdrop of foggy grey, with a few bright points gleaming through. I didn't know what it was intended to represent.

He handed me another; it was similar. So was the third, with the added detail that one rock fragment had a smooth side, with tiny lines across it. Winter spoke up. "The scale is not what it appears; that odd bit is a portion of the earth's crust, about twenty miles from the camera; the lines are roads." I stared, fascinated. Beyond the strangely scribed fragment, other jagged pieces ranged away to the limit of sight, and beyond. My imagination reeled at the idea that perhaps Winter was telling me the literal truth.

Winter passed over another shot. This one showed a lumpy black expanse, visible only by the murky gleam of light reflected by the irregularities in the surface in the direction of the moon, which showed as a brilliant disc in the black sky.

The next was half-obscured by a mass, which loomed across the lens, too close for focus. Beyond, a huge sprawling bulk, shapeless, gross, immense, lay half-buried in tangled vines. I stared horrified at the tiny cowlike head, which lolled uselessly on the slope of the mountainous creature. Some distance away a distended leg-like appendage projected, the hoof dangling.

"Yes," Winter said. "It's a cow. A mutated cow that no longer has any limitation on its growth. It's a vast tissue culture, absorbing nourishment direct from the vines. They grow all through the mass of flesh. The rudimentary head and occasional limbs are quite useless." I pushed the pictures back at him. I was sick. "I've seen enough," I said. "You've sold me. Let's get out of this." I pushed the pistol into my pocket. I thought of the bullet hole in the panel and shuddered.

Back in the office, I sat down at the desk. Winter spoke up again. "It's a very unnerving thing, old chap, to have it shown to you all at once that way."

Winter went on talking while I tried to assemble his fragmentary information into a coherent picture. A vast spider web of lines, each one a complete universe, each minutely different from all the others; somewhere, a line, or world, in which a device had been developed that enabled a man to move across the lines. Well, why not, I thought. With all those lines to work with, everything was bound to happen in one of them; or was it?

"How about all the other A-lines, Winter," I said at the thought, "where this same discovery must have been made, where there was only some unimportant difference. Why aren't you swarming all over each other, bumping into yourself?"

"That's been a big question to our scientists, old chap, and they haven't yet come up with any definitive answers. However, there are a few established points. First, the thing is a fantastically delicate device, as I've explained. The tiniest slip in the initial experimentation, and we'd have ended like some of those other lines you've seen photos of. Apparently the odds were quite fantastically against our escaping the consequences of the discovery; still, we did, and now we know how to control it.

"As to the very close lines, theory now seems to indicate that there is no actual physical separation between lines; those microscopically close to one another actually merge or blend. It's difficult to explain. One actually wanders from one to another, at random, you know. In fact, such is the curious nature of infinity, that there seem to be an infinite number of infinitely close lines we're constantly shifting about in. Usually this makes no difference; we don't notice it, any more than we're aware of hopping along from one temporal point to the next as normal entropy progresses."

At my puzzled frown he added, "The lines run both ways, you know, in an infinite number of directions. If we could run straight back along the normal E-line, we'd be travelling into the past. This won't work, for practical reasons involving two bodies occupying the same space, and all that sort of thing. The Maxoni principle enables us to move in a manner, which we think of as being at right angles to the normal drift. With it, we can operate through 360 degrees, but always at the same E-Level at which we start. Thus, we will arrive at Stockholm Zero Zero at the same moment we departed from B-I Three." Winter laughed. "This detail caused no end of misunderstanding and counter-accusation on the first trials."

"So we're all shifting from one universe to another all the time without knowing it," I said skeptically.

"Not necessarily all of us, not all the time," Winter said. "But emotional stress seems to have the effect of displacing one. Of course with the relative positions of two grains of sand, or even of two atoms within a grain of sand being the only difference between two adjacent lines, you'd not be likely to notice. But at times greater slips occur with most individuals. Perhaps you yourself have noticed some tiny discrepancy at one time or another; some article apparently moved or lost; some sudden change in the character of someone you know; false recollections of past events. The universe isn't all as rigid as one might like to believe."

"You're being awfully plausible, Winter," I said. "Let's pretend I accept your story. Now tell me about this vehicle."

"Just a small mobile ME station, mounted on an auto-propelled chassis. It can move about on level ground or paved areas, and also in calm water. It enables us to do most of our spatial maneuvering on our own ground, so to speak, and avoid the hazards of attempting to conduct ground operations in strange areas."

"Where are the rest of the men in your party?" I asked. "There are at least three more of you."

"They're all at their assigned posts," Winter said. "There's another small room containing the drive mechanism forward of the control compartment."

"What's this stuff for?" I indicated the box on the desk from which I'd gotten the gun.

Winter looked at it, then said ruefully, "So that's where you acquired the weapon. I knew you'd been searched. Damned careless of Doyle—bloody souvenir hunter! I told him to submit everything to me for approval before we returned, so I suppose it's my fault." He touched his aching hand tenderly.

"Don't feel too bad about it. I'm just a clever guy," I said. "However, I'm not very brave. As a matter of fact, I'm scared to death of what's in store for me when we arrive at out destination."

"You'll be well treated, Mr. Bayard," Winter assured me. I let that one pass. Maybe when we arrived, I could come out shooting, making an escape. That line of thought didn't seem very encouraging either. What would I do next, loose in this Imperium of Winter's? What I needed was a return ticket home. I found myself thinking of it as B-I Three, and realized I was beginning to accept Winter's story. I took a drink from the blue bottle.

"Why don't we explode when we pass through one of those empty-space lines, or burn in the hot ones?" I asked suddenly. "Suppose we found ourselves peeking out from inside one of those hunks of rock you were photographing?"

"We don't linger about long enough, old boy," Winter said. "We remain in anyone line for no finite length of time, therefore there's no time for us to react physically to our surroundings."

"How can you take pictures and use communicators?"

"The camera remains inside the field. The photo is actually a composite exposure of all the lines we cross during the instant of the exposure. The lines differ hardly at all, of course, and the prints are quite clear. Light, of course, is a condition, not an event. Our communicators employ a sort of grating which spreads the transmission."

"Winter," I said, "this is all extremely interesting, but I get the impression that you have small regard for a man's comfort. I think you might be planning to use me in some sort of colorful experiment, and then throw me away—toss me out into one of those cosmic junk heaps you showed me. And that stuff in the blue bottle isn't quite soothing enough to drive the idea out of my mind."

"Great heavens, old boy!" Winter sat bolt upright. "Nothing of that sort, I can assure you. Why, we're not blasted barbarians! Since you are an object of official interest of the Imperium, you can be assured of humane and honorable treatment."

"I didn't like what you said about concentration points a while back. That sounds like jail to me."

"Not at all," Winter expostulated. "There are a vast number of very pleasant A-lines well outside the Blight which are either completely uninhabited, or are occupied by backward or underdeveloped peoples. One can well nigh select the technological and cultural level in which one would like to live. All interrogation subjects are most scrupulously provided for; they're supplied with everything necessary to live in comfort for the remainder of their normal lives."

"Marooned on a desert island, or parked in a native village? That doesn't sound too jolly to me," I said. "I'd rather be at home."

Winter smiled speculatively. "What would you say to being set up with a fortune in gold, and placed in a society closely resembling that of, say, England in the seventeenth century with the added advantage that you'd have electricity, plenty of modern literature, supplies for a lifetime, whatever you wished. You must remember that we have all the resources of the universe to draw upon."

"I'd like it better if I had a little more choice," I said.

"Suppose we keep right on going, once we're clear of the Blight," I said. "That reception committee wouldn't be waiting then. You could run this buggy back to B-I Three. I could force you."

"See here, Bayard," Winter said impatiently. "You have a gun. Very well, shoot me; shoot all of us. What would that gain you? The operation of this machine requires a very high technical skill. The controls are set for automatic return to the starting point. It is absolutely against Imperium policy to return a subject to the line from which he was taken. The only thing for you to do is cooperate with us, and you have my assurance as an Imperial officer that you will be treated honorably."

I looked at the gun. "According to the movies," I said, "the fellow with the rod always gets his own way. But you don't seem to care whether I shoot you or not."

Winter smiled. "Aside from the fact that you've had quite a few draughts from my brandy flask and probably couldn't hit the wall with that weapon you're holding, I assure…"

"You're always assuring me," I said. I tossed the pistol onto the desk. I put my feet up on the polished top, and leaned back in the chair. "Wake me up when we get there. I'll want to fix my face."

Winter laughed. "Now you're being reasonable, old boy. It would be damned embarrassing for me to have to warn the personnel at base that you were waving a pistol about."

CHAPTER THREE

I WOKE up with a start. My neck ached abominably; so did the rest of me, as soon as I moved. I groaned, dragged my feet down off the desk, and sat up. There was something wrong. Winter was gone and the humming had stopped. I jumped up.

"Winter," I shouted. I had a vivid picture of myself marooned in one of those hell-worlds. At that moment I realized I wasn't half as afraid of arriving at Zero Zero as I was of not getting there.

Winter pushed the door open and glanced in. "I'll be with you in a moment, Mr. Bayard," he said. "We've arrived on schedule."

I was nervous. The gun was gone. I told myself it was no worse than going to one of the ambassador's receptions. My best bet was to walk in as though I'd thought of it myself.

The two bouncers came in, followed by Winter. One of the two men pushed the door open, and stood at attention beside it. Beyond the opening I could see muted sunshine on a level paved surface, and a group of men in white uniforms, looking in our direction.

I stepped down through the door and looked around. We were in a large shed, looking something like a railroad station. A group of men in white uniforms were waiting.

One of them stepped forward. "By Jove, Winter," he said. "You've brought it off. Congratulations, old man." The others came up, gathered around Winter, asking questions, turning to stare at me. None of them said anything to me. To hell with them, I thought. I turned and started strolling toward the front of the shed. There was one door with a sentry box arrangement beside it. I gave the man on duty a glance and started past.

"You'd better memorize this face," I said coolly. "You'll be seeing a great deal of it from now on. I'm your new commander." I looked him up and down. "Your uniform is in need of attention." I turned and went on.

Winter appeared at that point, putting an end to what would have been a very neat escape. But where the hell would I have gone?

"Here, old man," he said. "Don't go wandering about. I'm to take you directly to Royal Intelligence, where you'll doubtless find out a bit more about the reasons for your, ah—" Winter cleared his throat, "visit."

"I thought it was Imperial Intelligence," I said. "And for the high level operation this supposed to be, this is a remarkably modest reception. I thought there would be a band, or at least a couple of cops with handcuffs."

"Royal Swedish Intelligence," Winter explained briskly. "Sweden will bring tributary to the Emperor, of course. Imperial Intelligence chaps will be on hand. As for your reception, we don't believe in making much fuss, you know." Winter waved me into a boxy black staff car, which waited at the curb. It swung out at once into light traffic, which pulled out of our way as we rode down the center of the broad avenue.

"I thought your scout just travelled cross-ways," I said, "and stayed in the same spot on the map. This doesn't look like the hilly area of the Old Town."

"You have a suspicious mind and an eye for detail," Winter said. "We maneuvered the scout through the streets to the position of the ramps before going into drive. We're on the north side of the city now."

Our giant car roared across a bridge, and swirled into a long gravel drive leading to a wrought-iron gate before a massive grey granite building. The people I saw looked perfectly ordinary, with the exception of a few oddities of dress and an unusually large number of gaudy uniforms. The guard at the iron gate was wearing a cherry-colored tunic, white trousers, and a black steel helmet surmounted by a gold spike and a deep purple plume. He presented arms—a short and wicked looking nickel-plated machine gun—and as the gate swung wide we eased past him and stopped before broad doors of polished ironbound oak. A brass plate beside the entrance said Kungliga Svenska Spionage.

I said nothing as we walked down a spotless white marble-floored hall, entered a spacious elevator, and rode up to the top floor. We walked along another hall; this one paved with red granite, and paused before a large door at the end. There was no one else around.

"Just relax, Mr. Bayard. Answer all questions fully, and use the same forms of address as I do."

"I'll try not to fall down," I said. Winter looked as nervous as I felt as he opened the door after a polite tap.

The room was an office, large and handsomely furnished. Across a wide expanse of grey rug three men sat around a broad desk, behind which sat a fourth. Winter closed the door, walked across the room with me trailing behind him, and came to a rigid position of attention ten feet from the desk. His arms swung up in a real elbow-buster of a salute and held it.

"Sir, Chief Captain Winter reports as ordered," he said in a strained voice.

"Very good, Winter," said the man behind the desk, sketching a salute casually. Winter brought his arm down with a snap. He rotated rigidly toward the others.

"Kaiserliche Hochheit," he said, bowing stiffly from the waist at one of the seated figures. "Chief Inspector," he greeted the second, while the third, a rather paunchy fellow with a jolly expression and a somehow familiar face, rated just "Sir."

"'Hochwelgeboren' will do," murmured the lean aristocratic-looking one whom Winter had addressed first. Apparently instead of an imperial highness he was only a high-well-born. Winter turned bright pink. "I beg your Excellency's pardon," he said in a choked voice. The round-faced man grinned broadly.

The man behind the desk had been studying me intently during this exchange. "Please be seated, Mr. Bayard," he said pleasantly, indicating an empty chair directly in front of the desk. Winter was still standing rigidly. The man glanced at him. "Stand at ease, Chief Captain," he said in a dry tone, turning back to me.

"I hope that your being brought here has not prejudiced you against us unduly, Mr. Bayard," he said. He had a long gaunt face with a heavy jaw.

"I am General Bernadotte," he went on. "These gentlemen are the Friherr von Richthofen, Chief Inspector Bale, and Mr. Goering." I nodded at them. Bale was a thin broad-shouldered man with a small bald head. He wore an expression of disapproval.

Bernadotte went on. "I would like first to assure you that our decision to bring you here was not made lightly. I know that you have many questions, and all will be answered fully. For the present, I shall tell you frankly that we have called you here to ask for your help."

I hadn't been prepared for this. I don't know what I expected, but to have this panel of high-powered brass asking for my puny assistance left me opening and closing my mouth without managing to say anything.

"It's remarkable," commented the paunchy civilian. I looked at him. Winter had called him Mr. Goering. I thought of pictures of Hitler's gross Air Chief.

"Not Hermann Goering?" I said.

The fat man looked surprised, and a smile spread across his face.

"Yes, my name is Hermann," he said. "How did you know this?" He had a fairly heavy German accent.

I found it hard to explain. This was something I hadn't thought of—actual doubles or analogs of figures in my own world. Now I knew beyond a doubt that Winter had not been lying to me.

"Back where I came from, everyone knows your name," I said. "Reichmarshall Goering…"

"Reichmarshall!" Goering repeated. "What an intriguing title!" He looked around at the others. "Is this not a most interesting and magnificent information?" He beamed. "I, poor fat Hermann, a Reichmarshall, and known to all." He was delighted.

"Multi-phased reality is, of course, rather a shocking thing to encounter suddenly," the general said, "after a lifetime of living in one's own narrow world. To those of us who have grown up with it, it seems only natural and in keeping with the principles of multiplicity and the continuum. The idea of a monolinear casual sequence is seen to be an artificially restrictive conception, an oversimplification of reality growing out of human egotism."

The other four men listened as attentively as I. It was very quiet, with only the occasional faint sounds of traffic from the street below.

"Insofar as we have been able to determine thus far from our studies of the B-I Three line, from which you come, our two lines share a common history up to about the year 1790. They remain parallel in many ways for about another century; thereafter they diverge rather sharply.

"Here in our world, two Italian scientists, Giulio Maxoni and Carlo Cocini, in the year 1893, made a basic discovery, which, after several years of study, they embodied in a device which enabled them to move about at will through a wide range of what we now term Alternative lines, or A-lines.

"Cocini lost his life in an early exploratory test, and Maxoni determined to offer the machine to the Italian government. He was rudely rebuffed.

"After several years of harassment by the Italian press, which ridiculed him unmercifully, Maxoni went to England, and offered his invention to the British government. There was a long and very cautious period of negotiation, but eventually a bargain was struck. Maxoni received a title, estates, and one million pounds in gold. He died a year later.

"The British government now had sole control of the most important basic human discovery since the wheel. The wheel gave man the power to move easily across the surface of his world; the Maxoni principle gave him all the worlds to move about in."

Leather creaked faintly as I moved in my chair. The general leaned back and drew a deep breath. He smiled.

"I hope that I am not overwhelming you with an excess of historical detail, Mr. Bayard."

"Not at all," I replied. "I'm very much interested."

He went on. "At that time the British government was negotiating with the Imperial Germanic government in an effort to establish workable trade agreements, and avoid a fratricidal war, which then appeared to be inevitable if appropriate spheres of influence were not agreed upon.

"The acquisition of the Maxoni papers placed a different complexion on the situation. Rightfully feeling that they now had a considerably more favorable position from which to negotiate, the British suggested an amalgamation of the two empires into the present Anglo-Germanic Imperium, with the House of Hanover-Windsor occupying the Imperial throne. Sweden signed the Concord shortly thereafter, and after the resolution of a number of differences in detail, the Imperium came into being on January 1, 1900."

I had the feeling the general was over-simplifying things. I wondered how many people had been killed in the process of resolving the minor details. I kept the thought to myself.

"Since its inception," the general continued, "the Imperium has conducted a program of exploration, charting, and study of the A-continuum. It was quickly determined that for a vast distance on all sides of the home line, utter desolation existed; outside that blighted region, however, were the infinite resources of countless lines. Those lines lying just outside the Blight seem uniformly to represent a divergence point at about 400 years in the past; that is to say, our common histories differentiate about the year 1550. As one travels further out, the divergence date recedes. At the limits of our explorations to date the CH dated is about 1,000,000 B.C."

I didn't know what to say, so I said nothing. This seemed to be all right with Bernadotte.

"Then, in 1947, examination of photos made by automatic camera scouts revealed an anomaly; an apparently normal, inhabited world, lying well within the Blight. It took weeks of careful searching to pinpoint the line. For the first time, we were visiting a world closely analogous to our own, in which many of the institutions of our own world should be duplicated.

"We had hopes of a fruitful liaison between the two worlds, but in this we were bitterly disappointed."

The general turned to the bald man whom he had introduced as Chief Inspector Bale.

"Chief Inspector," he said, "will you take up the account at this point?"

Bale sat up in his chair, folded his hands, and began.

"In September 1948 two senior agents of Imperial Intelligence were dispatched with temporary rank of Career Minister and full diplomatic accreditation, to negotiate an agreement with the leaders of the National People's State. This political unit actually embraces most of the inhabitable world of the B-I Two line. A series of frightful wars, employing some sort of radioactive explosives, had destroyed the better part of civilization.

"Europe was a shambles. We found that the NPS headquarters was in North Africa, and had as its nucleus the former French colonial government there. The top man was a ruthless ex-soldier who had established himself as uncontested dictator of what remained of things. His army was made up of units of all the previous combatants, held together by the promise of free lotting and top position in a new society based on raw force.

"Our agents approached a military sub-chief, calling himself Colonel-General Yang, in charge of a ragtag mob of ruffians in motley uniforms, and asked to be conducted to the headquarters of the dictator. Yang had them clapped into a cell and beaten insensible in spite of their presentation of diplomatic passports and identity cards.

"He did however send them along to the dictator to have an interview. During the talk, the fellow drew a pistol and shot one of my two chaps through the head, killing him instantly. When this failed to make the other volunteer anything further than that he was an accredited envoy of the Imperial government requesting an *exequatur* and appropriate treatment, prior to negotiating an international agreement, he was turned over to experienced torturers.

"Under torture, the agent gave out just enough to convince his interrogators that he was insane; he was released to starve or die of wounds. We managed to spot him and pick him up in time to get the story before he died."

I still had no comment to make. It didn't sound pretty, but then I wasn't too enthusiastic about the methods employed by the Imperium either. The general resumed the story.

"We resolved to make no attempt at punitive action, but simply to leave this unfortunate line in isolation.

"About a year ago, an event occurred which rendered this policy no longer tenable." Bernadotte turned to the lean-faced man.

"Manfred, I will ask you to cover this part of the briefing."

"Units of our Net Surveillance Service detected activity at a point some distance within the area called Sector 92," Richthofen began. "This was a contingency against which we had been on guard from the first. A heavily armed ME unit of unknown origin had dropped into identity with one of our most prized industrial lines, one of a group with which we conduct a multi-billion pound trade. The intruder materialized in a population center, and released virulent poisonous gases, killing hundreds. Masked troops then emerged, only a platoon or two of them, and proceeded to strip bodies, loot shops—an orgy of wanton destruction. Our NSS scout arrived some hours after the attackers had departed. The scout, in turn, was subjected to a heavy attack by the justifiably aroused inhabitants of the area before it was able to properly identify itself as an Imperium vessel."

Richthofen had a disdainful frown on his face. "I personally conducted the rescue and salvage operation; over four hundred innocent civilians dead, valuable manufacturing facilities destroyed by fire, production lines disrupted, the population entirely demoralized. A bitter spectacle for us."

"You see, Mr. Bayard," Bernadotte said, "we are well nigh helpless to protect our friends against such forays. Although we have developed extremely effective ME field detection devices, the difficulty of reaching the scene of an attack in time is practically insurmountable. The actual transit takes no time, but locating the precise line among numerous others is an extremely delicate operation. Our homing devices make it possible, but only after we have made a very close approximation manually."

"In quick succession thereafter," Richthofen continued, "we suffered seven similar raids. Then the pattern changed. The raiders began appearing in numbers, with large cargo carrying units. They also set about rounding up all the young women at each raid, and taking them along into captivity. It became obvious that a major threat to the Imperium had come into existence.

"At last we had the good fortune to detect a raider's field in the close vicinity of one of our armed scouts. It quickly dropped in on a converging course, and located the pirate about twenty minutes after it had launched its attack. The commander of the scout quite properly opened up at once with high explosive cannon and blew the enemy to rubble. Its crew, although demoralized by the loss of their vessel, nevertheless resisted capture almost to the last man. We were able to secure only two prisoners for interrogation."

I wondered how the Imperium's method of interrogation compared with those of the dictator of B-I Two, but I didn't ask. I might find out soon enough.

"We learned a great deal more than we expected from our prisoners. They were the talkative, boastful type. The effectiveness of the raiding parties depended on their striking unexpectedly and departing quickly. The number of pirate vessels was placed at no more than four, each manned by about fifty men. They boasted of a great weapon held in reserve, and which would be used to avenge them. It was apparent from the remarks of the prisoners that they had not had the MC drive long, and that they knew nothing of the configuration of the Net, or of the endless ramifications of simultaneous reality.

"They seemed to think their fellows would find our base and destroy it with ease. They also had only a vague idea of the extent and nature of the Blight. They mentioned that several of their ships had disappeared, doubtless into that region. It appears also, happily for us, that they have only the most elementary detection devices and that their controls are erratic in the extreme. But the information of real importance was the identity of the raiders."

Richthofen paused for dramatic effect. "It was our unhappy sister world, B-I Two."

"Somehow," Bernadotte took up the story, "in spite of their condition of chaotic social disorder and their destructive wars, they had succeeded in harnessing the MC principle. Their apparatus is even more primitive than that with which we began almost sixty years ago; yet they have escaped disaster.

"The next move came with startling suddenness. Whether by virtue of an astonishingly rapid scientific development, or by sheer persistence and blind luck, one of their scouts succeeded, last month, in locating the Zero Zero line of the Imperium itself. The vessel dropped into identity with our continuum on the outskirts of the city of Berlin, one of the royal capitals.

"The crew had apparently been prepared for their visit. They planted a strange device atop a flimsy tower in a field, and embarked instantly. Within a matter of three minutes, as well as we have been able to determine, the device detonated with unbelievable force. Over a square mile was absolutely desolated; casualties ran into the thousands. And the entire area still remains poisoned with some form of radiation-producing debris which renders the region uninhabitable."

I nodded. "I think I understand," I said.

"Yes," the general said, "you have something of this sort in your B-I Three world also, do you not?"

I assumed the question was rhetorical and said nothing.

Bernadotte continued. "Crude though their methods are, they have succeeded already in flaunting the Imperium. It is only a matter of time, we feel, before they develop adequate controls and detection devices. We will then be faced with the prospect of hordes of ragged but efficient soldiers, armed with the frightful radium bombs with which they destroyed their own culture, descending on the mother world of the Imperium.

"This eventuality is one for which it has been necessary to make preparation. There seemed to be two possibilities, both equally undesirable. We could await further attack, meanwhile readying our defenses, of doubtful value against the fantastic explosives of the enemy; or we could ourselves mount an offensive, launching a massive invasion force against B-I Two. The logistics problems involved in either plan would be unbelievably complex."

I was learning a few things about the Imperium. In the first place, they did not have the atomic bomb, and had no conception of its power. Their consideration of war against an organized military force armed with atomics was proof of that. Also, not having had the harsh lessons of two major wars to assist them, they were naive, almost backward, in some ways. They thought more like Europeans of the nineteenth century than modern westerners.

"About one month ago, Mr. Bayard," Bale took over, "a new factor was introduced, giving us a third possibility. In the heart of the Blight, at only a very little distance from B-I Two, and even closer to us than it, we found a second surviving line. That line was of course your home world, designated Blight-Insular Three.

"Within seventy-two hours one hundred and fifty special agents had been placed at carefully scouted positions in B-I Three. We were determined to make no blunders; too much was at stake. As the information flowed in from our men, all of whom, being top agents, had succeeded in establishing their cover identities without difficulty, it was immediately passed to the General Staff and to the Imperial Emergency Cabinet for study. The two bodies remained in constant session for over a week without developing any adequate scheme for handling the new factor.

"One committee of the Emergency Cabinet was assigned the important task of determining as closely as possible the precise CH relationship of B-I Three with both B-I Two and the Imperium. This is an extremely tricky chore as it is quite possible for an amazing parallelism to exist in one phase of an A-line while the most fantastic variants crop up in another.

"One week ago today the committee reported findings they considered to be ninety-eight percent reliable. Your B-I Three line shared history of the B-I Two until the date 1911, probably early in the year. At that point, my colleague, Mr.

Goering, of German Intelligence, who had been sitting in on the meeting, made a brilliant contribution. His suggestion was immediately adopted. All agents were alerted at once to drop all other lines of inquiry and concentrate on picking up a trace of—" Bale looked at me.

"Mr. Brion Bayard."

They knew I was on the verge of exploding from pure curiosity, so I just sat and looked back at Bale. He pursed his lips. He sure as hell didn't like me.

"We picked you up from records at your university—" Bale frowned at me. "Something like aluminum alloy..."

Bale must be an Oxford man, I thought.

"Illinois," I said.

"At any rate," Bale went on, "it was a relatively simple matter to follow you up then through your military service and into your Diplomatic Service. Our man just missed you at your Legation at Viat-Kai."

"Consulate General," I corrected.

It annoyed Bale. I was glad; I didn't like him much either.

"You had left the post the preceding day and were proceeding to your headquarters via Stockholm. We had a man on the spot; he kept tabs on you until the shuttle could arrive. The rest you know."

There was a lengthening silence. I shifted in my chair, looking from one expressionless face to another.

"All right," I said. "It seems I'm supposed to ask, so I'll oblige, just to speed things along. Why me?"

Almost hesitantly General Bernadotte opened a drawer of the desk and drew out a flat object wrapped in brown paper. He removed the paper very deliberately as he spoke.

"I have here an official portrait of the dictator of the world of Blight-Insular Two," he said. "One of the two artifacts we have been able to bring along from that unhappy region. Copies of this picture are posted everywhere there."

He passed it over to me. It was a crude lithograph, in color, showing a man in uniform, the chest as far down as the picture extended covered with medals. Beneath the portrait was the legend: His Martial Excellency, Duke of Algiers, Warlord of the Combined Forces, Marshal General of the State, Brion The First Bayard, Dictator."

The picture was of me.

CHAPTER FOUR

I STARED at the garish portrait for a long time. It wasn't registering; I had a feeling of disorientation. There was too much to absorb.

"Now you will understand, Mr. Bayard, why we have brought you here," the general said, as I silently handed the picture back to him. "You represent our hidden ace. But only if you consent to help us of your own free will." He turned to Richthofen again.

"Manfred, will you outline our plan to Mr. Bayard?"

Richthofen cleared his throat. "Quite possibly," he said, "we could succeed in disposing of the Dictator Bayard by bombing his headquarters. This, however, would merely create a temporary diversion until a new leader emerged. The organization of the enemy seems to be such that no more than a very brief respite would be gained, if any at all, before the attacks would be resumed; and we are not prepared to sustain such onslaughts as these.

"No, it is far better for our purpose that Bayard remain the leader of the National People's State—and that we control him." Here he looked intently at me.

"A specially equipped TNL scout, operated by our best pilot technician, could plant a man within the private apartment which occupies the top floor of the dictator's palace at Algiers. We believe that a resolute man introduced into the palace in this manner, armed with the most effective hand weapons at our disposal, could succeed in locating and entering the dictator's sleeping chamber, assassinating him, and disposing of the body.

"If that man were you, Mr. Bayard, fortified by ten days' intensive briefing and carrying a small net-communicator, we believe that you could assume the identity of the dead man and rule as absolute dictator over Bayard's twenty million fighting men."

"Do I have another double here," I said, "in your Imperium?"

Bernadotte shook his head. "No, you have remote cousins here, nothing closer."

They all watched me. I could see that all three of them expected me to act solemn and modest at the honor, and set out to do or die for the fatherland. They were overlooking a few things, though. This wasn't my fatherland; I'd been kidnapped and brought here. And oddly enough, I could not see myself murdering anybody—especially, I had the grotesque thought—myself. I didn't even like the idea of being dropped down in the midst of a pack of torturers.

I was ready to tell them so in very definite terms, when my eye fell on Bale. He was wearing a supercilious half-smile, and I could see that this was just what he expected. His contempt for me was plain. I sensed that he thought of me as the man who had killed his best agent in cold blood, a cowardly blackguard. My mouth was open to speak; but under that sneering expression, different words came out— temporizing words. I wouldn't give Bale the satisfaction of being right.

"And after I'm in charge of B-I Two, what then?" I said.

"You will be in constant touch with Imperial Intelligence via communicator," Richthofen said eagerly. "You'll receive detailed instructions as to each move to make. We should be able to immobilize B-I Two within six months. You'll then be returned here."

"I won't be returned home?"

"Mr. Bayard," Bernadotte said seriously, "you will never be able to return to B-I Three. The Imperium will offer you any reward you wish to name, except that. The consequences of revealing the existence of the Imperium to your line at this time are far too serious to permit consideration of the idea. However—"

All eyes were on Bernadotte. He looked as though what he was about to say was important.

"I have been authorized by the Emergency Cabinet," he said with gravity, "to offer you an Imperial commission in the rank of Major General, Mr. Bayard. If you accept this commission, your first assignment will be as we have outlined." Bernadotte handed a heavy piece of parchment across the table to me. "You should know, Mr. Bayard, that the Imperium does not award commissions, particularly that of General Officer, lightly."

"It will be a most unusual rank," Goering said, smiling. "Normally there is no such rank in the Imperium Service; Lieutenant General, Colonel General, Major General. You will be unique."

"We adopted the rank from your own armed forces, as a special mark of esteem, Mr. Bayard," Bernadotte said. "It is no less authentic for being unusual."

It was a fancy sheet of paper. The Imperium was prepared to payoff well for this job they needed done—anything I wanted. And doubtless, they thought the strange look on my face was greed at the thought of a general's two stars. Well, let them think it. I didn't want to give them any more information, which might be used against me.

"I'll think about it," I said. Bale looked disconcerted now. After expecting me to back out, he had apparently then expected me to be dazzled by the reward I was being offered. I'd let him worry about it. Suddenly Bale bored me.

Bernadotte hesitated. "I'm going to take an unprecedented step, Mr. Bayard," he said. "For the present, on my personal initiative as head of State, I'm confirming you as Colonel in the Royal Army of Sweden without condition. I do this to show my personal confidence in you, as well as for more practical reasons." He rose and smiled ruefully, as though unsure of my reaction. "Congratulations, Colonel," he said, holding out his hand.

I stood up too. I noticed everyone had.

"You must have twenty-four hours to consider your decision, Colonel," he said. "I'll leave you in the excellent care of Graf von Richthofen and Mr. Goering until then."

Richthofen turned to Winter, still standing silently by. "Won't you join us, Chief Captain," he said.

"Delighted," Winter said.

"Congratulations, old boy, er, Sir," Winter said as soon as we were in the hall. "You made quite a hit with the general." He seemed quite his jaunty self again.

I eyed him. "You mean King Gustav?" I said.

Winter blinked. "But how did you know?" he said. "I mean dash it, how the devil did you know?"

"But it must be," Goering said with enthusiasm, "that also he in your home world is known, not so?"

"That's right, Mr. Goering," I said. "Now you've dispelled my aura of mystery."

Goering chuckled. "Please, Mr. Bayard, you must call me Hermann." He gripped my arm in friendly fashion as we moved down the hall. "Now you must tell us more about this intriguing world of yours."

Richthofen spoke up. "I suggest we go along to my summer villa at Drottningholm and enjoy a dinner and a couple of good vintages while we hear all about your home, Mr. Bayard; and we shall tell you of ours."

CHAPTER FIVE

I STOOD before a long mirror and eyed myself, not without approval. Two tailors had been buzzing around me like bees for half an hour, putting the finishing touches on their handiwork. I had to admit they had done all right.

I now wore narrow-cut riding breeches of fine grey whipcord, short black boots of meticulously stitched and polished black leather, a white linen shirt without collar or cuffs beneath a mess jacket of royal blue, buttoned to the chin. A gold-bordered blue stripe ran down the side of the trousers and heavy loops of gold braid ringed the sleeves from wrist to elbow. A black leather belt with a large square buckle bearing the Royal Swedish crest supported a jeweled scabbard containing a slender rapier with an ornate hilt.

In the proper position on the left side of the chest were, to my astonishment, a perfectly accurate set of my World War II Service medals and the Silver Star. On the shoulder straps, the bright silver eagles of a U.S. Colonel gleamed. I was wearing the full dress uniform of my new position in the Imperium society.

I was glad now I hadn't let myself deteriorate into the flabby ill-health of the average Foreign Service Officer, soft and pale from long hours in offices and late hours of heavy drinking at the interminable diplomatic functions. My shoulders were reasonably broad, my back reasonably straight, no paunch marred the lines of my new finery. This outfit made a man look like a man. How the devil had we gotten into the habit of draping ourselves in shapeless double-breasted suits, in mousy colors, of identical cut?

Goering was sitting in a brocaded armchair in the luxurious suite to which Richthofen had shown me in his villa.

"You cut a martial figure, Brion," he said. "It is plain to see you have, for this new job, a natural aptitude."

"I wouldn't count on it, Hermann," I said. His comment had reminded me of the other side of the coin; the deadly plans the Imperium had in mind for me. Well, I could settle that later. Tonight I was going to enjoy myself.

Over a dinner of pheasant served on a sunny terrace in the long Swedish summer evening, Richthofen had explained to me that, in Swedish society, to be without a title was an extremely awkward social encumbrance. It was not that one needed an exalted position, he assured me; merely that there must be something for others to call one—Herr Doctor, Herr Professor, Ingenjör, Redactor. My military status would ease my entry into the world of the Imperium.

Winter came in then, carrying what looked like a crystal ball.

"Your topper, sir," he said with a flourish. What he had was a chrome-plated steel helmet, with a rib running along the top, and a gold-dyed plume growing out of it.

"Good God," I said. "Isn't that overdoing it a little?" I took the helmet; it was feather light, I discovered. The tailor took over, placed the helmet just so, handed me a pair of white leather gloves, and faded out.

"You have to have it, old boy," Winter said. "Dragoons, you know.

"You are complete," Hermann said. "A masterpiece."

He was wearing a dark grey uniform with black trim and white insignia. He had a respectable but not excessive display of ribbons and orders.

"Hermann," I said expansively, "you should have seen yourself when you were all rigged out in your medals back home. They came down to here." I indicated my knees. He laughed.

Together we left the suite and went down to the study on the ground floor. Winter, I noted, had changed from his whites to a pale yellow mess jacket with heavy silver braid and a nickel-plated Luger.

Richthofen showed up moments later; his outfit consisted of what looked like a set of tails, circa 1880, with silver buttons and a white beret.

"We're a cool bunch of cats," I said. I was feeling swell. I caught another glimpse of myself in a mirror. "Sharp, daddy-o," I murmured.

A liveried butler swung the glass door open for us and we descended the steps to a waiting car. This one was a vast yellow phaeton, with the top down. We slid into our places on the smooth yellow leather seats and it eased off down the drive.

It was a magnificent night, with high clouds and a brilliant moon. In the distance, the lights of the city glittered. We rolled smoothly along, the engine so silent that the sound of the wind in the tall trees along the way was clearly audible.

Goering had thought to bring along a small flask, and by the time we had each tapped it twice we were passing through the iron gates of the summer palace. Colored floodlights bathed the gardens and people already filled the terrace on the south and west sides of the building. The car dropped us before the gigantic entry and moved off. We made our way through the crowd, and into the reception hall.

Light from massive crystal chandeliers glittered on gowns and uniforms, polished boots and jewels, silks, brocades and velvets. A straight-backed man in rose-pink bowed over the hand of a lovely blonde in white. A slender black-clad fellow with a gold and white sash escorted a lady in green-gold toward the ballroom. The din of laughter and conversation almost drowned out the strains of the waltz in the background.

"All right, boys," I said. "Where's the punch bowl?"

I don't often set out to get stewed, but when I do, I don't believe in half measures. I was feeling great, and wanted to keep it that way. At the moment, I couldn't feel the bruises from my fall, my indignation over being grabbed was forgotten, and as for tomorrow, I couldn't care less. I was having a wonderful time. I hoped I wouldn't see Bale's sour face.

Everybody talked, asked me eager questions, made introductions. I found myself talking to someone I finally recognized as Douglas Fairbanks, Sr. He was a tough-looking old fellow in a naval uniform. I met counts, dukes, officers of a dozen ranks I'd never heard of, several princes, and finally a short broad-shouldered man with a heavy suntan and a go-to-hell smile whom I finally realized was the son of the Emperor.

I was still walking and talking like a million dollars, but somewhere along the line I'd lost what little tact I normally had.

"Well, Prince William," I said, weaving just a little, "I understood the House of Hanover-Windsor was the ruling line here. Where I come from the Hanovers and the Windsors are all tall, skinny and glum-looking."

The Prince smiled. "Here, Colonel," he said, "a policy was established which put an end to that unfortunate situation. The Constitution requires that the male heir marry a commoner. This not only makes life more pleasant for the heir, with so many beautiful commoners to choose from, but maintains the vigor of the line. And it incidentally produces short men with happy faces occasionally."

I moved on, meeting people, eating little sandwiches, drinking everything from aquavit to beer, and dancing with one heavenly-looking girl after another. For the first time in my life my ten years of Embassy elbow-bending were standing me in good stead. From the grim experience gained through seven evenings a week of holding a drink in my hand from sundown till midnight while pumping other members of the Diplomatic Corps who thought they were pumping me, I had emerged with a skill; I could hold my liquor.

Somewhere along the line I felt the need for a breath of fresh air and stepped out through the tall French doors onto a dark balustraded gallery overlooking the gardens. I leaned on the heavy stone rail, looked up at the stars visible through tall treetops, and waited for the buzzing in my head to die down a little.

The night air moved in a cool torrent over the dark lawn, carrying the scent of flowers. Behind me the orchestra played a tune that was almost, but not quite, a Strauss waltz.

I pulled off the white gloves that Richthofen had told me I should keep on when I left my helmet at the checkroom. I unbuttoned the top button of the tight-fitting jacket.

I'm getting old, I thought, or maybe just tired.

"And why are you tired, Colonel?" a cool feminine voice inquired from behind me.

I turned around. "Ah, there you are," I said. "I'm glad. I'd rather be guilty of talking out loud than of imagining voices."

I worked on focusing my eyes a little better. She had red hair, and wore a pale pink gown that started low and stayed with the subject.

"I'm very glad, as a matter of fact," I added. "I like beautiful redheads who appear out of nowhere."

"Not out of nowhere, Colonel," she said. "From in there, where it is so warm and crowded."

She spoke excellent English in a low voice, with just enough Swedish accent to render her tritest speech charming.

"Precisely," I said. "All those people were making me just a little bit drunk, so I came out here to recover." I was wearing a silly smile, and having a thoroughly good time being so eloquent and clever with this delightful young lady.

"My father has told me that you are not born to the Imperium, Colonel," she said. "And that you come from a world where all is the same, yet different. It should be so interesting to hear about it."

"Why talk about that place?" I said. "We've forgotten how to have fun back there. We take ourselves very seriously, and we figure out the most elaborate excuses for doing the rottenest things to each other..."

I shook my head. I didn't like that train of thought. "See," I said, "I always talk like that with my gloves off." I pulled them on again. "And now," I said grandly, "may I have the pleasure of this dance?"

It was half an hour before we went back inside to visit the punchbowl. The orchestra had just begun a waltz when a shattering blast rocked the floor, and the tall glass doors along the east side of the ballroom blew in. Through the cloud of dust, which followed up the explosion, a swarm of men in motley remnants of uniforms leaped into the room. The leader, a black-bearded giant wearing a faded and patched U.S. Army-type battle jacket and baggy Wehrmacht trousers, jacked the lever on the side of a short drum-fed machine gun, and squeezed a long burst into the thick of the crowd.

Men and women alike fell under the murdering attack, but every man who remained on his feet rushed the nearest attacker without hesitation. Standing in the rubble, a bristle-faced redhead wearing an undersized British sergeant's blouse pumped eight shots from the hip, knocking down an oncoming officer of the Imperium with every shot; when he stepped back to jam a new clip into the M-I, the ninth man ran him through the throat with a jewel-encrusted rapier.

I still stood frozen, holding my girl's hand. I whirled, started to shout to her to get back, to run; but the calm look I saw in her eyes stopped me. She'd rather be decently dead than flee this rabble.

I jerked my toy sword from its scabbard, dashed to the wall, and moved along it to the edge of the gaping opening. As the next man pushed through the cloud of dust and smoke, peering ahead, gripping a shotgun, I jammed the point of my sword into his neck, hard, and jerked it back before it was wrenched from my hands. He stumbled on, choking, the shotgun falling with a clatter. I reached out, raked it in, as another man appeared. He carried a Colt .45 in his left hand, and he saw me as I saw him. He swiveled to fire, and as he did I brought the poised blade down on his arm. The shot went into the floor and the pistol bounced out of the loose hand. He fell back into the trampling crowd.

Another fellow lunged out of the dust, cutting across the room, and saw me. He leveled a heavy rifle on its side across his left forearm. He moved slowly and clumsily. I saw that his left hand was hanging by a thread. I grabbed up the shotgun and blew his face off. It had been about two minutes since the explosion.

I waited a moment, but no more came through the blasted window. I saw a wiry ruffian with long yellow hair falling back toward me as he pushed another magazine into a Browning automatic rifle. I jumped two steps, set the point of the sword just about where the kidneys should be, and rammed with both hands. Not very elegant style, I thought, but I'm just a beginner.

I saw Goering then, arms around a tall fellow who cursed and struggled to raise his battered sub-machine gun. A gun roared in my ear and the back of my neck burned. I realized my jump had literally saved my neck. I ran around to the side of the grappling pair, and shoved the blade into the thin man's ribs. It grated and stuck, but he wilted. I'm not much of a sport, I thought, but I guess guns against pig-stickers makes it even.

Hermann stepped back, spat disgustedly, and leaped on the nearest bandit. I wrenched at my sword, but it was wedged tight. I left it and grabbed up the tommy gun. A long-legged villain was just closing the chamber of his revolver as I pumped a burst into his stomach. I saw dust fly from the shabby cloth of his coat as the slugs smacked home.

I glanced around. Several of the men of the Imperium were firing captured guns now, and the remnant of the invading mob had fallen back toward the shattered wall. Bullets cut them down as they stood at bay, still pouring out a ragged fire. None of them tried to flee.

I ran forward, sensing something wrong. I raised my gun and cut down a bloody-faced man as he stood firing two .45 automatics. My last round nicked a heavy-set carbine man, and the drum was empty. I picked up another weapon from the floor, as one lone thug still standing pounded the bolt of his rifle with his palm.

"Take him alive," someone shouted. The firing stopped and a dozen men seized the struggling man. The crowd milled, women bending over those who lay on the floor, men staggering from their exertions. I ran toward the billowing drapes.

"Come on," I shouted. "Outside..." I didn't have time or breath to say more, or to see if anyone came. I leaped across the rubble, out onto the blasted terrace, leaped the rail, and landed in the garden, sprawled a little, but still moving. In the light of the colored floods a grey-painted van, ponderously bulky, sat askew across flowerbeds. Besides it, three tattered crewmen struggled with a bulky load. A small tripod stood on the lawn, awaiting the mounting of their burden. I had time for one momentary mental vision of what a fission bomb would do to the summer palace and its occupants, before I dashed at them with a yell. I fired the pistol I had grabbed, as fast as I could pull the trigger, and the three men hesitated, pulled against each other, cursed, and started back toward the open door of their van with the bomb. One of them fell, and I realized someone behind me was firing accurately. Another of the men yelped and ran off a few yards to crumple on the grass. The third jumped for the open door, and a moment later a rush of air threw dust against my face as the van flicked out of existence. The sound was like a pool of gasoline igniting.

The bulky package lay on the ground now, ominous. I felt sure it was not yet armed. I turned to the others. "Don't touch this thing," I called. "I'm sure it's some kind of atomic bomb."

"Nice work, old boy," a familiar voice said. It was Winter, blood spattered on the pale yellow of his tunic. "Might have known those chaps were fighting a delaying action for a reason. Are you all right?"

"Yeah," I said, breathless. "Let's go back inside. They'll need tourniquets and men to twist them."

We picked our way through the broken glass, fragments of flagstones, and splinters of framing, past the flapping drapes, into the brightly lit dust-rolled ballroom.

Dead and wounded lay in a rough semicircle around the broken wall. I recognized a pretty brunette in a blue dress whom I had danced with earlier, lying on the floor, face waxen. Everyone was splattered with crimson. I looked around frantically for my redhead, and saw her kneeling beside a wounded man, binding his head.

There was a shout. Winter and I whirled. One of the wounded intruders moved, threw something, then collapsed as shots struck him. I heard the thump and the rattle as the object fell, and as in a dream I watched the grenade roll over and over, clattering, stop ten feet away and spin a half turn. I stood, frozen. Finished, I thought. And I never even learned her name.

From behind me I heard a gasp as Winter leaped past me and threw himself forward. He landed spread-eagled over the grenade as it exploded with a muffled thump, throwing Winter two feet into the air.

I staggered, and turned away, dizzy. Poor Winter. Poor damned Winter.

I felt myself passing out, and went to my knees. The floor was tilting.

She was bending over me, face pale, but still steady.

I reached up and touched her hand. "What's your name?" I said.

"My name?" she said. "Barbro Lundane. I thought you knew my name." She seemed a bit dazed. I sat up. "Better lend a hand to someone who's worse off than I am, Barbro," I said. "I just have a weak constitution."

"No," she said. "You've bled much."

Richthofen appeared, looking grim. He helped me up. My neck and head ached. "Thank God you are alive," he said.

"Thank Winter I'm alive," I replied. "I don't suppose there's a chance...?"

"Killed instantly," Richthofen said. "He knew his duty."

"Poor guy," I said. "It should have been me."

"We're fortunate it wasn't you," Richthofen said. "It was close. As it is, you've lost considerable blood. You must come along and rest now."

"I want to stay here," I said. "Maybe I can do something useful."

Goering had appeared from somewhere, and he laid an arm across my shoulders, leading me away.

"Calmly, now, my friend," he said. "There is no need to feel it so strongly; he died in performance of his duty, as he would have wished."

Hermann knew what was bothering me. I could have blanked out that grenade as easily as Winter, but the thought hadn't even occurred to me. If I hadn't been paralyzed, I'd have run.

I didn't struggle; I felt washed out, suddenly suffering a premature hangover. Manfred joined us at the car, and we drove home in near silence. I asked about the bomb and Goering said that Bale's men had taken it over. "Tell them to dump it at sea," I said.

At the villa, someone waited on the steps as we drove up. I recognized Bale's rangy figure with the undersized head. I ignored him as he collared Hermann.

I went into the dining room, poured a stiff drink at the sideboard, sat down.

The others came behind me, talking. I wondered where Bale had been all evening.

Bale sat down, eyeing me. He wanted to hear all about the attack. He seemed to take the news calmly but sourly.

He looked at me, pursing his lips. "Mr. Goering has told me that you conducted yourself quite well, Mr. Bayard, during the fight. Perhaps I was hasty in my judgment of you."

"Who the hell cares what you think, Bale?" I said. "Where were you when the lead was flying? Under the rug?"

Bale turned white, stood up glaring and stalked out of the room. Goering cleared his throat and Manfred cast an odd look at me as he rose to perform his hostly duty of conducting a guest to the door.

"Inspector Bale is not a man easy to associate with," Hermann said. "I understand your feeling." He rose and came around the table.

"I feel you should know," he went on, "that he is among the most skillful with sabre and epee. Make no hasty decision now—"

"What decision?" I asked.

"Already you have a painful wound," he said. "We must not allow you to be laid up at this critical time. Are you sure, of your skill with a pistol?"

"What wound?" I said. "You mean my neck?" I put my hand up to touch it. I winced; there was a deep gouge, caked with blood. Suddenly I was aware that the back of my jacket was soggy. That near miss was a little nearer than I had thought.

"I hope you will accord Manfred and myself the honor of seconding you," Hermann continued, "and perhaps of advising you…"

"What's this all about, Hermann?" I said. "What do you mean—seconding me?"

"Why," he seemed confused, "we wish to stand with you in your meeting with Bale."

"Meeting with Bale?" I repeated. I knew I didn't sound very bright. I was beginning to realize how lousy I felt.

Goering stopped and looked at me. "Inspector Bale is a man most sensitive of personal dignity," he said. "You have given him a tongue-lashing before witnesses, and a well deserved one it was; however, it remains a certainty that he will demand satisfaction." He saw that I was still groping. "Bale will challenge you, Brion," he said. "You must fight him."

CHAPTER SIX

I WAS cold, chilled to the bone. I was still half asleep, and I carried my head tilted forward and a little to the side in a hopeless attempt to minimize the vast throbbing ache from the furrow across the back of my neck.

Richthofen, Goering and I stood together under spreading linden trees at the lower end of the Royal Game Park. It was a few minutes before dawn and I was wondering how a slug in the kneecap would feel.

There was the faint sound of an engine approaching, and a long car loomed up in the gloom on the road above, lights gleaming through morning mist.

The sound of doors opening and slamming was muffled and indistinct. Three figures were dimly visible, approaching down the gentle slope. My seconds moved away to meet them. One of the three detached itself from the group and stood alone, as I did. That would be Bale.

Another car pulled in behind the first. The doctor, I thought. In the dim glow from the second car's small square cowl lights I saw another figure emerge. I watched; it looked like a woman.

I heard the murmur of voices, a low chuckle. They were very palsy, I thought. Everything on a very high plane.

I thought over what Goering had told me on the way to the field of honor, as he called it.

Bale had offered his challenge under the Toth convention. This meant that the duelists must not try to kill each other; the object of the game was to inflict painful wounds, to humiliate one's opponent.

This could be a pretty tricky business. In the excitement of the fight, it wasn't easy to inflict wounds that were thoroughly humiliating but definitely not fatal.

Richthofen had lent me a pair of black trousers and a white shirt for the performance, and a light overcoat against the pre-dawn chill. I wished it had been a heavy one. The only warm part of me was my neck, swathed in bandages.

The little group broke up now. My two backers approached, smiled encouragingly, and in low voices invited me to come along. Goering took my coat. I missed it.

Bale and his men were walking toward a spot in the clear, where the early light was slightly better. We moved up to join them.

"I think we have light enough now, eh, Baron?" said Hallendorf.

I could see better now; the light was increasing rapidly. Long pink streamers flew in the east; the trees were still dark in silhouettes.

Hallendorf stepped up to me, and offered the pistol box.

I picked one of the pistols, without looking at it. Bale took the other, methodically worked the action, snapped the trigger, examined the rifling. Richthofen handed each of us a magazine.

"Five rounds," he said. I had no comment.

Bale stepped over to the place indicated by Hallendorf and turned his back. I could see the cars outlined against the sky now. The big one looked like a '30 Packard, I thought. At Goering's gesture, I took my post, back to Bale.

"At the signal, gentlemen," Hallendorf said, "step forward ten paces and pause; at the command turn and fire. Gentlemen, in the name of the Emperor and of honor!"

The white handkerchief in his hand fluttered to the ground. I started walking. One, two, three…

There was someone standing by the smaller car. I wondered who it was…eight, nine, ten. I stopped, waiting. Hallendorf's voice was calm. "Turn and fire."

I turned, holding the pistol at my side. Bale pumped a cartridge into the chamber, set his feet apart, body sideways to me, left arm behind his back, and raised his pistol. We were seventy feet apart across the wet field.

I started walking toward him. Nobody had said I had to stay in one spot. Bale lowered his pistol slightly and I saw his pale face, eyes staring. The pistol came up again and almost instantly jumped as a flat crack rang out. The spent cartridge popped up over Bale's head and dropped on the wet grass, catching the light. A miss.

I walked on. I had no intention of standing in the half dark, firing wildly at a half-seen target. I didn't intend to be forced into killing a man by accident, even if it was his idea. And I didn't intend to be pushed into solemnly playing Bale's game with him.

Bale held the automatic at arm's length, following me as I approached. He could have killed me easily, but that was against the code. The weapon wavered; he couldn't decide on a target. My moving was bothering him.

The pistol steadied and jumped again, the shot sounding faint on the foggy air. I realized he was trying for the legs; I was close enough now to see the depressed angle of the barrel.

He stepped back a pace, set himself again, and raised the Mauser higher. He was going to try to break a rib, I guessed. A tricky shot, easy to miss—either way. My stomach muscles tensed with anticipation.

I didn't hear the next one; the sensation was exactly like a baseball bat slammed against my side. I felt that I was stumbling, air knocked from my lungs, but I kept my feet. A great warm ache spread from just above the hip. Only twenty feet away now. I fought to draw a breath.

Bale's expression was visible, a stiff shocked look, mouth, squeezed shut. He aimed at my feet and fired twice in rapid succession; I think by error. One shot went through my boot between the toes of my right foot, the other in the dirt. I walked up to him. I sucked air in painfully. I wanted to say something, but I couldn't. It was all I could do to keep from gasping. Abruptly, Bale backed a step, aimed the pistol at my chest and pulled the trigger; it clicked. He looked down at the gun.

I dropped the Mauser at his feet, doubled my fist, and hit him hard on the jaw. He reeled back as I turned away. I walked over to Goering and Richthofen as the doctor hurried up. They came forward to meet me.

"Lieber Gott," Hermann breathed as he seized my hand, and pumped it. "This story they will never believe."

"If your object was to make a fool of Inspector Bale," Richthofen said with a gleam in his eye, "you have scored an unqualified success. I think you have taught him respect."

The doctor pressed forward. "Gentlemen, I must take a look at the wound." A stool was produced, and I gratefully sank down on it.

I stuck my foot out. "Better take a look at this too," I said, "it feels a little tender."

The doctor muttered and exclaimed as he began snipping at the cloth and leather. He was enjoying every minute of it. The doc, I saw, was a romantic.

A thought was trying to form itself in my mind. I opened my eyes. Barbro was coming toward me across the grass, dawn light gleaming in her red hair. I realized what it was I had to say.

"Hermann," I said. "Manfred. I need a long nap, but before I start I think I ought to tell you; I've had so much fun tonight that I've decided to take the job."

"Easy, Brion," Manfred said. "There's no need to think of it now."

"No trouble at all," I said.

Barbro bent over. "Brion," she said. "You are not badly hurt?" She looked worried.

I smiled at her and reached for her hand. "I'll bet you think I'm accident prone; but actually I sometimes go for days at a time without so much as a bad fall."

She took my hand in both of hers as she knelt down. "You must be suffering great pain, Brion, to talk so foolishly," she said. "I thought he would lose his head and kill you." She turned to the doctor. "Help him, Dr. Blum."

"You are fortunate, Colonel," the doctor said, sticking a finger into the furrow on my side. "The rib is not fractured. In a few days you will have only a little scar and a big bruise to remind you."

I squeezed Barbro's hand. "Help me up, Barbro," I said.

Goering gave me his shoulder to lean on. "For you now, a long nap," he said. I was ready for it.

CHAPTER SEVEN

I TRIED to relax in my chair in the cramped shuttle. Just in front of me the operator sat tensed over a tiny illuminated board, peering at instrument faces and tapping the keys of what looked like a miniature calculating machine. A soundless hum filled the air, penetrating my bones.

I twisted, seeking a more comfortable position. My half-healed neck and side were stiffening up again. Bits and fragments of the last ten days' incessant briefing ran through my mind. Imperial Intelligence hadn't been able to gather as much material as they wanted on Marshal of the State Bayard, but it was more than I was able to assimilate consciously. I hoped the hypnotic sessions I had had every night for a week in place of real sleep had taken at a level where the data would pop up when I needed it.

Bayard was a man of mystery, even to his own people. He was rarely seen, except via what the puzzled Intelligence men said seemed to be a sort of electric picture apparatus. I had tried to explain that TV was commonplace in my world, but they never really understood it.

They had given me a good night's sleep the last three nights, and a tough hour of cleverly planned calisthenics every day. My wounds had healed well, so that now I was physically ready for the adventure; mentally, however, I was fagged. The result was an eagerness to get on with the thing and find out the worst of what I was faced with. I had enough of words; now I wanted the relief of action.

I checked over my equipment. I wore a military tunic duplicating that shown in the official portrait of Bayard. Since there was no information on what he wore below the chest, I had suggested olive drab trousers, matching what I recognized as the French regulation jacket.

At my advice, we'd skipped the ribbons and orders shown in the photo; I didn't think he would wear them around his private apartment in an informal situation. For the same reason, my collar was unbuttoned and my tie loosened.

They had kept me on a diet of lean beefsteak, to try to thin my face a bit. A hair specialist had given me vigorous scalp massages every morning and evening, and insisted that I not wash my head. This was intended to stimulate rapid growth and achieve the unclipped continental look of the dictator's picture.

Snapped to my belt was a small web pouch containing my communication transmitter. We had decided to let it show rather than seek with doubtful success to conceal it. The microphone was woven into the heavy braid on my lapels. I had a thick stack of NPS currency in my wallet.

I moved my right hand carefully, feeling for the pressure of the release spring that would throw the palm-sized slug-gun into my hand with the proper flexing of the wrist.

The little weapon was a marvel of compact deadliness. In shape it resembled a water-washed stone, grey and smooth. It could lie unnoticed on the ground, a feature that might be of great importance to me in an emergency.

Inside the gun a hair-sized channel spiraled down into the grip. A compressed gas, filling the tiny hole, served as both propellant and projectile. At a pressure on the right spot, unmarked, a minute globule of the liquefied gas was fired with tremendous velocity. Once free of the confining walls of the tough alloy barrel, the bead expanded explosively to a volume of a cubic foot. The result was an almost soundless blow, capable of shattering one-quarter inch armor, instantly fatal within a range of ten feet.

It was the kind of weapon I needed—inconspicuous, quiet, and deadly at short range. The spring arrangement made it almost a part of the hand, if the hand were expert.

I had practiced the motion for hours, while listening to lectures, eating, even lying in bed. I was very conscientious about that piece of training; it was my insurance. I tried not to think about my other insurance, set in the hollowed-out bridge replacing a back tooth.

Each evening, after the day's hard routine, I had relaxed with new friends, exploring the Imperial Ballet, theatres, opera and a lively variety show. With Barbro, I had dined sumptuously at half a dozen fabulous restaurants and afterwards walked in moonlit gardens, sipped coffee as the sun rose, and talked. When the day came to leave, I had more than a casual desire to return. The sooner I got started, the quicker I would get back.

The operator turned. "Colonel," he said, "brace yourself, sir. There's something here I don't understand."

I tensed, but said nothing. I figured he would tell me more as soon as he knew more. I moved my hand tentatively against the slug-gun release. I already had the habit.

"I've detected a moving body in the Net," he said. "It seems to be trying to match our course. My spatial fix on it indicates it's very near."

The Imperium was decades behind my world in nuclear physics, television, aerodynamics, etc., but when it came to the instrumentation of these Maxoni devices, they were fantastic. After all, they had devoted their best scientific efforts to the task for almost sixty years.

Now the operator hovered over his panel controls like a nervous organist.

"I get a mass of about fifteen hundred kilos," he said. "That's about right for a light scout, but it can't be one of ours..."

There was a tense silence for several minutes.

"He's pacing us, Colonel," the operator said. "Either they've got better instrumentation than we thought, or this chap has had a stroke of blind luck. He was lying in wait."

Both of us were assuming the stranger could be nothing but a B-I Two vessel.

The operator tensed up suddenly, hands frozen. "He's coming in on us, Colonel," he said. "He's going to ram. We'll blow sky-high if he crosses our fix."

My thoughts ran like lightning over my slug-gun—the hollow tooth; I wondered what would happen when he hit. Somehow, I hadn't expected it to end here. The impossible tension lasted only a few seconds. The operator relaxed.

"Missed," he said. "Apparently his spatial maneuvering isn't as good as his Net mobility. But he'll be back; he's after blood."

I had a thought. "Our maximum rate is controlled by the energy of normal entropy, isn't it?" I asked.

He nodded.

"What about going slower," I said. "Maybe he'll overshoot."

I could see the sweat start on the back of his neck from here.

"A bit risky in the Blight, sir," he said, "but we'll have a go at it."

I knew how hard that was for an operator to say. This young fellow had had six years of intensive training, and not a day of it has passed without a warning against any unnecessary control changes in the Blight.

The sound of the generators changed, the pitch of the whine descending into the audible range, dropping lower.

"He's still with us, Colonel," the operator said.

The pitch fell lower. I didn't know when the critical point would be reached that we would lose our artificial orientation and rotate into normal entropy. We sat rigid, waiting. The sound dropped down, almost baritone now. The operator tapped again and again at a key, glancing at a dial.

The drive hum was a harsh droning now; we couldn't expect to go much further without disaster. But then neither could the enemy.

"He's right with us, Colonel, only—" Suddenly the operator shouted. "We lost him, Colonel! His controls aren't as good as ours in that line, anyway; he dropped into identity."

I sank back, as the whine of our MC generator built up again. My palms were wet. I wondered into which of the hells of the Blight they had gone. But I had another problem to face in a few minutes. This was not the time for shaken nerves.

"Good work, operator," I said at last. "How much longer?"

"About—good God—ten minutes, sir," he answered. "That little business took longer than I thought."

I started a last minute check. My mouth was dry. Everything seemed to be in place. I pressed the button on my communicator.

"Hello, Talisman," I said, "here is Wolfhound Red. How do you hear me? Over."

"Wolfhound Red, Talisman here, you're coming in right and bright, over." The tiny voice spoke almost in my ear from the speaker in a button on my shoulder strap.

I liked the instant response; I felt a little less lonesome.

I looked at the trip mechanism for the escape door. I was to wait for the operator to say, "Crash out," and hit the lever. I had exactly two seconds then to pull my arm back and kick the slug-gun into my palm before the seat would automatically dump me, standing, out the exit. The shuttle would be gone before my feet hit the floor.

I had been so wrapped up in the business at hand for the past ten days that I had not really thought about the moment of my arrival in the B-I Two world. The smoothly professional handling of my hasty training had given the job an air of practicality and realism. Now, about to be propelled into the innermost midst of the enemy, I began to realize the suicidal aspects of the mission. But it was too late now for second thoughts—and in a way I was glad. I was involved now in this world of the Imperium; it was a part of my life worth risking something for.

I was a card the Imperium held, and it was my turn to be played. I was valuable property, but that value could only be realized by putting me into the scene in just this way, and the sooner the better. I had no assurance that the dictator was in residence at the palace now; I might find myself hiding in his quarters awaiting his return, for God knows how long—and maybe lucky at that, to get that far. I hoped our placement of the suite was correct, based on information gotten from the captive taken at the ballroom, under deep narco-hypnosis. Otherwise, I might find myself treading air, 150 feet up.

There was a slamming of switches, and the operator twisted in his chair.

"Crash out, Wolfhound," he cried, "and good hunting."

Reach out and slam the lever; arm at the side, snap the gun into place in my hand; with a metallic whack and a rush of air the exit popped and a giant hand palmed me out into dimness. One awful instant of vertigo, of a step missed in the dark, and then my feet slammed against carpeted floor. Air whipped about my face, and the echoes of the departing boom of the shuttle still hung in the corridor.

I remembered my instructions. I stood still, turning casually to check behind me. There was no one in sight. The hall was dark except for the faint light from a ceiling fixture at the next intersection. I had arrived.

I slipped the gun back into its latch under my cuff. No point in standing here; I started off at a leisurely pace toward the light. The doors lining the hall were identical, unmarked. I paused and tried one. Locked. So was the next. The third one opened, and I looked cautiously into a sitting room. I went on. What I wanted was the sleeping room of the dictator, if possible. If he were in, I knew what to do; if not, presumably he would return if I waited long enough. Meanwhile, I wanted very much not to meet anyone.

There was the sound of an elevator door opening, just around the corner ahead. I stopped. I eased back to the last door I had checked, opened it and stepped inside, closing it almost all the way behind me. My heart was thudding painfully. I didn't feel daring; I felt like a sneak thief. Faintly, I heard steps coming my way.

I silently closed the door, taking care not to let the latch click. I stood behind it for a moment before deciding it would be better to conceal myself, just in case. I glanced around, moving into the center of the room. I could barely make out outlines in the gloom. There was a tall shape against the wall—a wardrobe, I thought. I hurried across to it, opened the door, and stepped in among hanging clothes.

I stood for a moment, feeling foolish, then froze as the door to the hall opened and closed again softly. There were no footsteps, and then a light went on. My closet door was open just enough to catch a glimpse of a man's back as he turned away from the lamp. I heard the soft sound of a chair being pulled out, and then the tiny jingle of keys. There were faint metallic sounds, a pause, more faint metallic sounds. The man was apparently trying keys in the lock of a table or desk.

I stood absolutely rigid. I breathed shallowly, tried not to think about a sudden itch on my cheek. I could see the shoulder of the coat hanging to my left. I turned my eyes to it. It was almost identical with the one I was wearing. The lapels were adorned with heavy braid. I had a small moment of relief; I had found the right apartment, at least. But my victim must be the man in the room; and I had never felt less like killing anyone in my life.

The little sounds went on. I could hear the man's heavy breathing. All at once I wondered what he would look like, this double of mine. Would he really resemble me, or more to the point, did I look enough like him to take his place?

I wondered why he took so long finding the right key; then another thought struck me. Didn't this sound a little more like someone trying to open someone else's desk? I moved my head a fraction of an inch. The clothes moved silently, and I edged a little farther. Now I could see him. He sat hunched in the chair, working impatiently on the lock. He was short and had thin hair, and resembled me not in the least. It was not the dictator.

This was a new factor for me to think over, and in a hurry. The dictator was obviously not around, or this fellow would not be here attempting to rifle his desk. And the dictator had people around him who were not above prying. That fact might be useful to me.

It took him five minutes to find a key that fit. I stood with muscles aching from the awkward pose, trying not to think of the lint that might cause a sneeze. I could hear the shuffling of papers and faint muttering as the man looked over his finds. At length there was the sound of the drawer closing, the click of the lock. Now the man was on his feet, the chair pushed back, and then silence for a few moments. Steps came toward me. I froze, my wrist twitching, ready to cover him and fire if necessary the instant he pulled the door open. I wasn't ready to start my imposture just yet skulking in a closet.

I let out a soundless sigh as he passed the opening and disappeared. More sounds as he ran through the drawers of a bureau or chest.

Suddenly the hall door opened again, and another set of steps entered the room. I heard my man freeze. Then he spoke, in guttural French.

"Oh, it's you, is it, Maurice."

There was a pause. Maurice's tone was insinuating.

"Yes, I thought I saw a light in the chief's study. I thought that was a bit odd, what with him away tonight."

The first man sauntered back toward the center of the room. "I just thought I'd have a look to see that everything was OK here."

Maurice tittered. "Don't try to rob a thief, Georges; I know why you came here—for the same reason as I."

"What are you up to?" the first man hissed. "What do you want?"

"Sit down, Flic. Oh, don't get excited; they all call you that." Maurice was enjoying himself. I listened carefully for half an hour while he goaded and cajoled, and pressured the other. The first man, I learned, was Georges Pinay, the chief of the dictator's security force. The other man was a civilian military adviser to the Bureau of Propaganda and Education. Pinay, it seemed, had been less clever than he thought in planning a coup that was to unseat Bayard. Maurice knew all about it, and had bided his time; and now he was taking over. Pinay didn't like it, but he accepted it after Maurice mentioned a few things nobody was supposed to know about; a hidden airplane and a deposit of gold coins buried a few miles outside the city.

I listened carefully, without moving, and after a while even the itch went away. Pinay had been looking for lists of names, he admitted; he planned to enlist a few more supporters by showing them their names in the dictator's own hand on the purge schedule. He hadn't planned to mention that he himself had nominated them for the list.

I made the mistake of over-confidence; I was just waiting for them to finish up when a sudden silence fell. I didn't know what I had done wrong, but I knew at once what was coming. The steps were very quiet and there was just a moment's pause before the door was flung open. I hoped my make-up was on straight.

I stepped out, casting a cool glance at Pinay.

"Well, Georges," I said, "it's nice to know you keep yourself occupied when I'm away." I used the same French dialect they had used, and my wrist was against the little lever.

"The devil," Maurice burst out. He stared at me with wide eyes. For a moment I thought I was going to get away with it. Then Pinay lunged at me. I whirled, side-stepped; and the slug-gun slapped my palm.

"Hold it," I barked.

Pinay ignored the order and charged again. I squeezed the tiny weapon, bracing myself against the recoil. There was a solid thump and Pinay bounced aside, landed on his back, loose-limbed, and lay still. Then Maurice hit me from the side. I stumbled across the room, tripped and fell, and he was on top of me. I still had my gun, and tried to bring it into play, but I was dazed, and Maurice was fast and strong as a bull. He flipped me and held me in a one-handed judo hold that pinned both arms behind me. He was astride me, breathing heavily.

"Who are you?" he hissed.

"I thought you'd know me, Maurice," I said. With infinite care I groped, tucked the slug-gun into my cuff. I heard it click home and I relaxed.

"So you thought that, eh?" Maurice laughed. His face was pink and moist. He pulled a heavy blackjack from his pocket as he slid off me. "Get up," he said. He looked me over.

"My God," he said. "Fantastic. Who sent you?"

I didn't answer. It seemed I wasn't fooling him for a minute. I wondered what was so wrong. Still, he seemed to find my appearance interesting. He stepped forward and slammed the sap against my neck, with a controlled motion. He could have broken my neck with it, but what he did was more painful. I felt the blood start from my half-healed neck; wound. He saw it, and looked puzzled for a moment. Then his face cleared.

"Excuse me," he said, grinning. "I'll try for a fresh spot next time. And answer when spoken to." There was a viciousness in his voice that reminded me of the attack at the palace. These men had seen hell on earth and they were no longer fully human.

He looked at me appraisingly, slapping his palm with the blackjack. "I think we'll have a little talk downstairs," he said. "Keep the hands in sight." His eyes darted about, apparently looking for my gun. He was very sure of himself; he didn't let it worry him when he didn't see it. He didn't want to take his eyes off me long enough to really make a search.

"Stay close, Baby," he said. "Just like that, come along now, nice and easy."

I kept my hands away from my sides, and followed him over to the phone. He wasn't as good as he thought; I could have taken him any time. I had a hunch, though, that it might be better to string along a little, to find out something more.

Maurice picked up the phone, spoke softly into it and dropped it back in the cradle. His eyes stayed on me.

"How long before they get here?" I asked.

Maurice narrowed his eyes, not answering.

"Maybe we have just time enough to make a deal," I said.

His mouth curved in what might have been a smile. "We'll make a deal all right, Baby," he said. "You sing loud and clear, and maybe I'll tell the boys to make it a fast finish."

"You've got an ace up your sleeve here, Maurice," I urged. "Don't let that rabble in on it."

He slapped his palm again. "What have you got in mind, Baby?"

"I'm on my own," I said. I was thinking fast. "I'll bet you never knew Brion had a twin brother. He cut me out, though, so I thought I'd cut myself in."

Maurice was interested. "The devil," he said. "You haven't seen your loving twin in a long time, I see." He grinned. I wondered what the joke was.

"Let's get out of here," I said. "Let's keep it between us two."

Maurice glanced at Pinay.

"Forget him," I said. "He's dead."

"You'd like that, wouldn't you, Baby?" Maurice said. "Just the two of us, and maybe then a chance to narrow it back down to one." His sardonic expression turned suddenly to a snarl, with nostrils flaring. "By God," he said, "you, you'd plan to kill me, you little man of straw—" He was leaning toward me now, arm loosening for a swing. I realized he was insane, ready to kill in an instantaneous fury.

"You'll see who is the killer between us," he said. His eyes gleamed as he swung the blackjack loosely in his hand.

I couldn't wait any longer. The gun popped into my hand, aimed at Maurice. I felt myself beginning to respond to his murder lust. I hated everything he stood for.

"You're stupid, Maurice," I said. "Stupid and slow, and in just a minute, dead. But first you're going to tell me how you knew I wasn't Bayard."

It was a nice try, but wasted.

Maurice leaped and the slug-gun slapped him aside. He hit and lay limp. My arm ached from the recoil. Handling the tiny weapon was tricky. It was good for about fifty shots on a charge; at this rate it wouldn't last a day.

I had to get out fast now. I reached up and smashed the ceiling light, then the table lamp. That might slow them up for a few moments. I eased out into the hall and started for the dark end. Behind me I heard the elevator opening. They were here already. I pushed at the glass door, and it swung open quietly. I didn't wait around to see what their reaction would be when they found Maurice and Georges. I went down the stairs two at a time, as softly as I could. I thought of my communicator and decided against it. I didn't have anything good to report.

I passed three landings before I emerged into a hall. This would be the old roof level. I tried to remember where the stair had come out in the analogous spot back at Zero Zero. I spotted a small door in an alcove; it seemed to be in about the right place.

A man came out of a room across the hall and glanced toward me. I rubbed my mouth thoughtfully, while heading for the little door. The resemblance was more of a hindrance than a help now. He went on, and I tried the door. It was locked, but it didn't look very strong. I put my hip against it and pushed. It gave way with no more than a mild splintering sound. The stairs were there, and I headed down.

I had no plan other than to get in the clear. It was obvious that the impersonation was a complete flop. All I could do was to get to a safe place and ask for further instructions. I had gone down two flights when I heard the alarm bell start.

I stopped dead. I had to get rid of the fancy uniform. I pulled off the jacket, then settled for tearing the braid off the wrists, and removing the shoulder tabs. I couldn't ditch the lapel braid; my microphone was woven into it. I couldn't do much else about my appearance.

This unused stair was probably as good a way out as any. I kept going. I checked the door at each floor. They were all locked. That was a good sign, I thought. The stair ended in a cul-de-sac filled with barrels and mildewed paper cartons. I went back up to the next landing and listened. Beyond the door there were loud voices and the clatter of feet. I remembered that the entry to the stair was near the main entrance to the old mansion. It looked like I was trapped.

I went down again, pulled one of the barrels aside. I peered behind it at the wall. The edge of a doorframe was visible. I maneuvered another barrel out of place and found the knob. It was frozen. I wondered how much noise I could make without being heard. Not much, I decided.

I needed something to pry with. The paper cartons looked like a possibility; I tore the flaps loose on one and looked in. It was filled with musty ledger books; no help.

The next was better. Old silverware, pots and pans. I dug out a heavy cleaver and slipped it into the crack. The thing was as solid as a bank vault. I tried again; it couldn't be that strong, but it didn't budge.

I stepped back. Maybe the only thing to do was forget caution and chop through the middle. I leaned over to pick the best spot to swing at—then jumped back flat against the wall, slug-gun in my hand. The doorknob was turning.

CHAPTER EIGHT

I WAS close to panic; being cornered had that effect on me. I didn't know what to do. I had plenty of instructions on how to handle the job of taking over after I had succeeded in killing the dictator, but none to cover retreat after failure.

There was a creak, and dust sifted down from the top of the door. I stood as far back as I could get, waiting. I had an impulse to start shooting, but restrained it. Wait and see.

The door edged open a crack. I really didn't like this; I was being looked over, and could see nothing myself. At least I had the appearance of being unarmed; the tiny gun was concealed in my hand. Or was that an advantage? I couldn't decide.

I didn't like suspense. "All right," I said. "You're making a draft. In or out." I spoke in the gutter Parisian I had heard upstairs.

The door opened farther, and a grimy-faced fellow was visible beyond it. He blinked in the dim light, peered up the stairs. He gestured.

"This way, come on," he said in a hoarse whisper. I didn't see any reason to refuse under the circumstances. I stepped past the barrels and ducked through the low doorway. As the man closed the door, I slipped the gun back into its clip. I was standing in a damp stone-lined tunnel, lit by an electric lantern sitting on the floor. I stood with my back to it. I didn't want him to see my face yet, not in a good light.

"Who are you?" I asked.

The fellow pushed past me and picked up his lantern. He hardly glanced at me.

"I'm just a dumb guy," he said. "I don't ask no questions, I don't answer none. Come on."

I couldn't afford to argue the point so I followed him. We made our way along the hand-hewn corridor, then down a twisting flight of steps, to emerge into a dark windowless chamber. Two men and a dark-haired girl sat around a battered table where a candle spluttered.

"Call them in, Miche," my guide said. "Here's the pigeon."

Miche lolled back in his chair and motioned me toward him. He picked up what looked like a letter-knife from the table and probed between two back teeth while he squinted at me. I made a point not to get too close.

"One of the kennel dogs, by the uniform," he said. "What's the matter, you bit the hand that fed you?" He laughed humorously.

I said nothing. I thought I'd give him a chance to tell me something first if he felt like it.

"A ranker, too, by the braid," he said. "Well, they'll wonder where you got to." His tone changed. "Let's have the story," he said. "Why are you on the run?"

"Don't let the suit bother you," I said. "I borrowed it. But it seemed like the people up there disliked me on sight."

"Come on over here," the other man said. "Into the light." I couldn't put it off forever. I moved forward, right up to the table. Just to be sure they got the idea, I picked up the candle and held it by my face.

Miche froze, knife point in his teeth. The girl started violently and crossed herself. The other man stared, fascinated. I'd gone over pretty big. I put the candle back on the table and sat down casually in the empty chair.

"Maybe you can tell me," I said, "why they didn't buy it."

The second man spoke. "You just walked in like that, sprung it on them?"

I nodded.

He and Miche looked at each other.

"You got a very valuable property here, my friend," the man said. "But you need a little help. Chica, bring wine for our new friend here."

The girl, still wide-eyed, scuttled to a dingy cupboard and fumbled for a bottle, looking at me over her shoulder.

"Look at him sitting there, Gros," Miche said. "Now that's something."

"You're right that's something," Gros said. "If it isn't already loused up." He leaned across the table. "Now just what happened upstairs?" he said. "How long have you been in the palace? How many have seen you?"

I gave them a brief outline, leaving out my mode of arrival. They seemed satisfied.

"Only two seen his face, Gros," Miche said, "and they're out of the picture." He turned to me. "That was a nice bit of work, mister, knocking off Souvet; and nobody ain't going to miss Pinay neither. By the way, where's the gun? Better let me have it." He held out his hand.

"I had to leave it," I said. "Tripped and dropped it in the dark."

Miche grunted.

"The Boss will be interested in this," Gros said. "He'll want to see him."

Someone else panted up the stairs into the room. "Say, Chief," he began, "we make it trouble in the tower—" He stopped dead as he caught sight of me, and dropped into a crouch, utter astonishment on his face. His hand clawed for a gun at his hip, found none, as his eyes darted from face to face.

"What—what—"

Gros and Miche burst into raucous laughter, slapping the table and howling. "At ease, Spider," Miche managed. "Bayard's throwed in with us." At this even Chica snickered.

Spider still crouched. "OK, what's the deal?" he gasped. "I don't get it." He glared around the room, face white. He was scared stiff. Miche wiped his face, whooped a last time, hawked and spat on the floor.

"OK, Spider, as you were," he said. "This here's a ringer. Now you better go bring in the boys. Beat it."

Spider scuttled away. I was puzzled. Why did some of them take one startled look and relax, while this fellow was apparently completely taken in? I had to find out. There was something I was doing wrong.

"Do you mind telling me," I said, "what's wrong with the get-up?" Miche and Gros exchanged glances again.

"Well, my friend," Gros said, "it's nothing we can't take care of. Just take it easy, and we'll set you right. You wanted to step in and take out the Old Man, and sit in for him, right? Well, with the Organization behind you you're as good as in."

"What's the Organization?" I asked.

Miche broke in. "For now we'll ask the questions," he said. "What's your name? What's your play here?"

I looked from Miche to Gros. I wondered which one was the boss. "My name's Bayard," I said.

Miche narrowed his eyes as he rose and walked around the table. He was a big fellow with small eyes.

"I asked you what's your name, mister?" he said. "I don't usually ask twice."

"Hold it, Miche," Gros said. "He's right. He's got to stay in this part, if he's going to be good; and he better be plenty good. Let's leave it at that; he's Bayard."

Miche looked at me. "Yeah," he said, "you got a point." I had a feeling Miche and I weren't going to get along.

"Who's backing you, uh, Bayard?" Gros said.

"I play a lone hand," I said. "Up to now, anyway. But it seems I missed something. If your Organization can get me in, I'll go along."

"We'll get you in, all right," Miche said.

I didn't like the looks of this pair of hoodlums, but I could hardly expect high-toned company here. As far as I could guess, the Organization was an underground anti-Bayard party. The room seemed to be hollowed out of the walls of the palace. Apparently they ran a spying operation all through the building, using hidden passages.

More men entered the room now, some via the stair, others through a door in the far corner. Apparently the word had gone out. They gathered around, staring curiously, commenting to each other, but not surprised.

"These are the boys," Gros said, looking around at them. "The rats in the walls."

I looked them over, about a dozen piratical-looking toughs; Gros had described them well. I looked back at him. "All right," I said. "Where do we start?" These weren't the kind of companions I would have chosen, but if they could fill in the gaps in my disguise for me, and help me take over in Bayard's place, I could only be grateful for my good luck.

"Not so fast," Miche said. "This thing is going to take time. We got to get you to a layout we got out of town. We got a lot of work ahead of us."

"I'm here now," I said. "Why not go ahead today? Why leave here?"

"We got a little work to do on your disguise," Gros said, "and there's plans to make. How do we get the most out of this break and how do we make sure there's no wires on this?"

"And no double-cross," Miche added.

A hairy lout listening in the crowd spoke up.

"I don't like the looks of this stool, Miche. I don't like funny stuff. I say under the floor with him." He wore a worn commando knife in a sheath fixed horizontally to his belt buckle. I was pretty sure he was eager to use it.

Miche looked at me. "Not for now, Gaston," he said.

Gros rubbed his chin. "Don't get worried about Mr. Bayard, boys," he said. "We'll have our eyes on him." He glanced up at Gaston. "You might make a special effort along those lines, Gaston; but don't get ahead of yourself. Let's say if he has any kind of accident, you'll have a worse one."

The feel of the spring under my wrist was comforting. I felt that Gaston wasn't the only one in this crew who didn't like strangers.

"I figure time is important," I said. "Let's get moving."

Miche stepped over to me. He prodded my leg with his boot. "You got a flappy mouth, mister," he said. "Gros and me gives the orders around here."

"OK," Gros said. "Our friend has got a lot to learn, but he's right about the time. Bayard's due back here sometime tomorrow, so that means we get out today, if we don't want the Ducals all over the place on top of the regulars. Miche, get the boys moving. I want things folded fast and quiet, and good men on the stand-by crew."

He turned to me as Miche bawled orders to the men.

"Maybe you better have a little food now," he said. "It's going to be a long day."

I was startled. I had been thinking of it as night. I looked at my watch. It had been one hour and ten minutes since I had entered the palace. Doesn't time go fast, I thought to myself, when everyone's having fun.

Chica brought over a loaf of bread and a wedge of brown cheese from the cupboard, and placed them on the table with a knife. I was cautious.

"OK if I pick up the knife?" I asked.

"Sure," Gros said. "Go ahead." He reached under the table and laid a short-nosed revolver before him.

Miche came back to the table as I chewed on a slice of tough bread. It was good bread. I tried the wine. It wasn't bad. The cheese was good, too.

"You eat well," I said. "This is good."

Chica threw me a grateful smile. "We do all right," Gros said.

"Better get Mouth here out of that fancy suit," Miche said, jerking his head at me. "Somebody might just take a shot at that without thinking. The boys have got kind of nervous about them kind of suits."

Gros looked at me. "That's right," he said. "Miche will give you some other clothes. That uniform don't go over so big here."

I didn't like this development at all. My communicator was built into the scrambled eggs on my lapels. I had to say no and make it stick.

"Sorry," I said. "I keep the outfit. It's part of the act. I'll put a coat over it if necessary."

Miche put his foot against my chair and shoved; I saw it coming and managed to scramble to my feet instead of going over with the chair. Miche faced me.

"Strip, mister," he said. "You heard the man."

The men still in the room fell silent, watching. I looked at Miche. I hoped Gros would speak up. I couldn't see anything to be gained by this.

Nobody spoke. I glanced over at Gros. He was just looking at us.

Miche reached behind, brought out a knife. The blade snicked out. "Or do I have to cut it off you," he growled.

"Put the knife away, Miche," Gros said mildly. "You don't want to cut up our secret weapon here; and we want the uniform off all in one piece."

"Yeah," Miche said. "You got a point." He dropped the knife on the table and moved in on me. From his practiced crouch and easy shuffling step, I saw that he had been a professional.

I decided not to wait for him. I threw myself forward with my weight behind a straight left to the jaw. It caught Miche by surprise, slammed against his chin and rocked him back. I tried to follow up, catch him again while he was still off balance, but he was a veteran of too many fights. He covered up, back-pedalled, shook his head, and then flicked out with a right that exploded against my temple. I was almost out, staggering. He hit me again, square on the nose. Blood flowed.

I wouldn't last long against this bruiser. The crowd was still bunched at the far end of the room, moving this way, now, watching delightedly, calling encouragement to Miche. Gros still sat, and Chica stared from her place by the wall.

I moved back, dazed, dodging blows. I had only one chance and I needed a dark corner to try it. Miche was right after me. He was mad; he didn't like that smack on the jaw in front of the boys. That helped me. He forgot boxing and threw one haymaker after another. He wanted to floor me with one punch to retrieve his dignity. I dodged and retreated.

I moved back toward the deep shadows at the end of the room, beyond Chica's pantry. I had to get there quickly, before the watching crowd closed up the space.

Miche swung again, left, right. I heard the air whistle as his ham-like fist grazed me. I backed another step; almost far enough. Now to get between him and the rest of the room. I jumped in behind a wild swing, popped a stinging right off his ear, and kept going. I whirled, snapped the slug-gun into my hand, and as Miche lunged, I shot him in the stomach, faked a wild swinging attack as he bounced off the wall and fell full length at my feet. I slipped the gun back into my cuff and turned.

"I can't see," a man shouted. "Get some light down here." The mob pushed forward, forming a wide ring. They stopped as they saw that only I was on my feet.

"Miche is down," a man called. "The new guy took him."

Gros pushed his way through, hesitated, then walked over to the sprawled body of Miche. He squatted, beckoned to the man with the candle.

He pulled Miche over on his back, then looked closer, feeling for the heartbeat. He looked up abruptly, got to his feet.

"He dead," he said. "Miche is dead." He looked at me with a strange expression. "It's quite a punch you got, mister," he said.

"I tried not to use it," I said. "But I'll use it again if I have to."

"Search him, boys," Gros said. They prodded and slapped, everywhere but my wrist. "He's clean, Gros," a man said. Gros looked the body over carefully, searching for signs of a wound. Men crowded around him.

"No marks," he said at last. "Broken ribs, and it feels like something funny inside; all messed up." He looked at me. "He did it barehanded."

I hoped they would go on believing that. It was my best insurance against a repetition. I wanted them scared of me, and the ethics of it didn't bother me at all.

"All right," Gros called to the men. "Back on the job. Miche asked for it. He called our new man 'Mouth.' I'm naming him 'Hammer-hand.'"

I thought this was as good a time as any to push a little farther.

"You'd better tell them I'm taking over Miche's spot here, Gros," I said. "We'll work together, fifty-fifty."

Gros squinted at me. "Yeah, that figures," he said. I had a feeling he had mental reservations.

"And by the way," I added, "I keep the uniform."

"Yeah," Gros said. "He keeps the uniform." He turned back to the men. "We pull out of here in thirty minutes. Get moving."

There was a ragged streak of light showing at the end of the dark tunnel. Gros signalled a halt. The men bunched up, filling the cramped passage.

"Most of you never came this way before," he said. "So listen. We push out of here into the Street of the Olive Trees; it's a little side street under the palace wall. There's a dummy stall in front; ignore the old dame in it.

"Ease out one at a time, and move off east; that's to the right. You all got good papers. If the guy on the gate asks for them, show them. Don't get eager and volunteer. If there's any excitement behind, just keep going. We rendezvous at the Thieves' Market. OK—and duck the hardware."

He motioned the first man out, blinking in the glare as the ragged tarpaulin was pushed aside. After half a minute, the second followed. I moved close to Gros.

"Why bring this whole mob along?" I asked in a low voice. "Wouldn't it be a lot easier for just a few of us?"

Gros shook his head. "I want to keep my eye on these slobs," he said. "I don't know what ideas they might get if I left them alone a few days; and I can't afford to have this set-up poisoned. And I'm going to need them out at the country place. There's nothing they can do here while I'm not around to tell them."

It sounded fishy to me, but I let it drop. All the men passed by us and disappeared. There was no alarm.

"OK," Gros said. "Stay with me." He slipped under the mouldy hanging and I followed as he stepped past a broken-down table laden with pottery. An old crone huddled on a stool ignored us. Gros glanced out into the narrow dusty street, then pushed off into the crowd. We threaded our way through loud-talking, gesticulating customers, petty merchants crouched over fly-covered displays of food or dog-eared magazines, tottering beggars, grimy urchins. The dirt street was littered with refuse; starving dogs wandered listlessly through the crowd. No one paid the least attention to us. It appeared we'd get through without trouble.

Under a heavy cloak Gros had given me, I was sweating. Flies buzzed about my swollen face. A whining beggar thrust a gaunt hand at me. Gros ducked between two fat men engaged in an argument. As they moved, I had to sidestep and push past them. Gros was almost out of sight in the mob.

I saw a uniform suddenly, a hard-faced fellow in yellowish khaki pushing roughly through the press ahead. A chicken fluttered up, squawking in my face. There was a shout; people began milling, thrusting against me. I caught a glimpse of Gros, face turned toward the soldier, eyes wide in a pale face. He started to run. In two jumps the uniformed man had him by the shoulder, spun him around, shouting. A dog yelped, banged against my legs, scuttled away. The soldier's arm rose and fell, clubbing at Gros with a heavy riot stick.

Far ahead I heard a shot, and almost instantly another, close. Gros was free and running, blood on his head, as the soldier fell among the crowd. I darted along the wall, trying to overtake Gros, or at least keep him in sight. The crowd was opening, making way as he ran, pistol in hand. He fired again, the shot a faint pop in the mob noise.

Another uniform jumped in front of me, club raised; I shied, threw up an arm, as the man jumped back, saluted.

I caught the words, "Pardon, sir," as I went past him at a run. He must have caught a glimpse of the uniform I wore.

Ahead, Gros fell in the dust, scrambled to his knees, head down. A soldier stepped out of an alley, aimed, and shot him through the head. Gros lurched, collapsed, rolled on his back. The dust caked in the blood on his face. The crowd closed in. From the moment they spotted him, he didn't have a chance.

I stopped. I was trying to remember what Gros had told the men. I had made the bad mistake of assuming too much, thinking I would have Gros to lead me out of this. There was something about a gate; everyone had papers, Gros said. All but me. That was why they had had to come out in daylight, I realized suddenly. The gate probably closed at sundown.

I moved on, not wanting to attract attention by standing still. I tried to keep the cloak around me to conceal the uniform. I didn't want any more soldiers noticing it; the next one might not be in such a hurry.

Gros had told the men to rendezvous at the Thieves' Market. I tried to remember Algiers from a three-day visit years before; all I could recall was the Casbah and the well-lit streets of the European shopping section.

I passed the spot where a jostling throng craned to see the body of the soldier, kept going. Another ring surrounded the spot where Gros lay dead. Now there were soldiers everywhere, swinging their sticks carelessly, breaking up the mob. I shuffled, head down, dodged a backhanded swipe, found myself in the open. The street sloped up, curving to the left. There were still a few cobbles on this part, fewer shops and stalls. Wash hung from railings around tiny balconies above the street.

I saw the gate ahead. A press of people packed against it, while a soldier examined papers. Three more uniformed men stood by, looking toward the scene of the excitement.

I went on toward the gate. I couldn't turn back now. There was a new wooden watchtower scabbed onto the side of the ancient brick wall where the sewer drained under it. A carbon arc searchlight and a man with a burp gun slung over his shoulder were on top of it. I thought I saw one of the Organization men ahead in the crowd at the gate.

One of the soldiers was staring at me. He straightened, glanced at the man next to him. The other soldier was looking, too, now. I decided a bold front was the only chance. I beckoned to one of the men, allowing the cloak to uncover the front of the uniform briefly. He moved toward me, still in doubt. I hoped my battered face didn't look familiar.

"Snap it up, soldier," I said in my best *Ecole Militaire* tone; he halted before me, saluted. I didn't give him a chance to take the initiative.

"The best part of the catch made it through the gate before you fools closed the net," I snapped. "Get me through there fast, and don't call any more attention to me. I'm not wearing this flea-circus for fun." I flipped the cloak.

He turned and pushed through to the gate, and said a word to the other soldier, gestured toward me. The other man, wearing sergeant's stripes, looked at me.

I glared at him as I approached. "Ignore me," I hissed. "You foul this up and I'll see you shot."

I brushed past him, thrust through the gate as the first soldier opened it. I walked on, listening for a sound of a round snapping into the chamber of that burp gun on the tower. A goat darted out of an alley, stared at me. Sweat rolled down my cheek. There was a tree ahead, with a black shadow under it. I wondered if I'd ever get that far.

I made it, and breathed a little easier.

I still had problems, plenty of them. Right now I had to find the Thieves' Market. I had a vague memory of such a thing from the past, but I had no idea where it was. I moved along the road, past a weathered stuccoed building with a slatternly tavern downstairs and sagging rooms above, bombed out at the far end. The gate was out of sight now.

Ahead were more bomb-scarred tenements, ruins, and beyond open fields. There was a river in sight to the right. A few people were in view, moving listlessly in the morning heat. They seemed to ignore the hubbub within the walled town. I couldn't risk asking any of them for the place I sought; I didn't know who might be a police informer, or a cop, for that matter. They had been ready for us, I realized.

Gros wasn't as well hidden as he had thought. Probably the police could have cleared his outfit from the palace at any time; I suspected they had tolerated them against such a time as now. The ambush had been neat. I wondered if any of the boys had made it through the gate.

Apparently word had not gone out to be on the alert for a man impersonating an officer; I didn't know how much Maurice had said when he telephoned for his men, but my bluff at the gate indicated no one had been warned of my disguise.

I paused. Maybe my best bet would be to try the tavern, order a drink, try to pick up something. I saw nothing ahead that looked encouraging.

I walked back fifty feet to the doorless entrance of the bistro. There was no one in sight. I walked in, barely able to make out the positions of the tables and chairs in the gloom. The glassless windows were shuttered. I blinked, made out the shape of the bar. Outside the door, the dusty road glared white.

A hoarse-breathing fellow loomed up behind the bar. He didn't say anything.

"Red wine," I said.

He put a water glass on the bar and filled it from a tin dipper. I tasted it. It was horrible. I had a feeling good manners would be out of place here, so I turned and spat it on the floor.

I pushed the glass across the bar. "I want wine," I said. "Not what you wring out of the bar rag." I dropped a worn thousand franc note on the bar.

He muttered as he turned away, and was still muttering when he shuffled back with a sealed bottle and a wineglass. He drew the cork, poured my glass half full, and put the thousand francs in his pocket. He didn't offer me any change.

I tried it; it wasn't too bad. I stood sipping, and waited for my eyes to get used to the dim light. The bartender moved away and began pulling a pile of boxes, grunting hard.

I didn't have a clear idea of what to do if I did find the survivors of the Organization. At best I might find out what was wrong with the disguise, and use their channels to get back into the palace. I could always call for help on my communicator, and have myself set back inside via shuttle, but I didn't like the idea of risking that again. I had almost been caught arriving last time. The scheme couldn't possibly work if any suspicion was aroused.

A man appeared in the doorway, silhouetted against the light. He stepped in and came over to the bar. The bartender ignored him.

Two more came through the door, walked past me and leaned on the bar below me. The bartender continued to shuffle boxes, paying no attention to his customers. I started to wonder why.

The man nearer me moved closer. "Hey, you," he said. He jerked his head toward the gate. "You hear the shooting back there?"

That was a leading question. I wondered if the sound of the shots had been audible outside the walls of the fortified town. I grunted.

"Who they after?" he said.

I tried to see his face, but it was shadowed. He was a thin broad fellow, leaning on one elbow. Here we go again, I thought.

"How would I know?" I said.

"Kind of warm for that burnoose, ain't it?" he said. He stretched out a hand as if to touch the tattered cape. I stepped back, and two pairs of arms wrapped around me in a double bear hug from behind.

The man facing me twitched the cape open. He looked at me.

"Lousy Ducal," he said, and hit me across the mouth with the back of his hand. I tasted blood.

"Hold on to them arms," another man said, coming around from behind me. This was one I hadn't seen. I wondered how many more men were in the room. The new man took the old military cape in his hands and ripped it off me.

"Look at that," he said. "We got us a lousy general." He dug his finger under the top of the braided lapel of my blouse and yanked. The lapel tore but stayed put. I started to struggle then; that was my communicator they were about to loot for the gold wire on it. I didn't have much hope of getting loose that way, but maybe it would distract them if I kicked a little. I swung a boot and caught the rangy one under the kneecap. He yelped and jumped back, then swung at my face. I twisted away, and the blow grazed my cheek. I threw myself backward, jerking hard, trying to throw someone off balance.

"Hold him," a man hissed. They were trying not to make too much noise. The thin man moved in close, watched his chance and slammed a fist into my stomach. The pain was agonizing; I cramped up, retching.

The men holding me dragged me to a wall, flung me upright against it, arms outspread. The fellow who wanted the braid stepped up with a knife in his hand. I was trying to breathe, wheezing and twisting. He grabbed my hair, and for a moment I thought he was going to slit my throat. Instead, he sawed away at lapels, cursing as the blade scraped wire.

"Get the buttons, too, Beau Joe," a husky voice suggested. The pain was fading a little now, but I sagged, acting weaker than I actually was. The communicator was gone, at least the sending end. All I could try to salvage now was my life.

The buttons took only a moment. The man with the knife stepped back, slipping it into a sheath at his hip. He favored the leg I had kicked. I could see his face now. He had straight fine features.

"OK, let him go," he said. I slumped to the floor. For the first time my hands were free. Now maybe I had a chance; I still had the gun. I got shakily to hands and knees, watching him. He aimed a kick at my ribs.

"On your feet, General," he said. "I'll teach you to kick your betters."

The others laughed, called out advice, shuffled around us in a circle. There was an odor of dust and sour wine.

"That General's a real fighter, ain't he?" somebody called. "Fights sittin' down." That went over big. Lots of happy laughter.

I grabbed the foot as it came to me, twisted it hard, and threw the man to the floor. He swore loudly, lunged at me, but I was up again, backing away. The ring opened and somebody pushed me. I let myself stumble and gained a few more feet toward the shadowed corner. I could see better now, enough to see pistols and knives in every belt. If they had any idea I was armed, they'd use them. I had to wait.

Beau Joe was after me again, throwing a roundhouse left. I ducked it, then caught a couple of short ones. I stepped back two paces, glanced at the audience; they were as far away as I'd get them. It was time to make my play. The man shielded me as the slug-gun popped into my hand, but at that instant he swung a savage kick. It was just luck; he hadn't seen the tiny weapon, but the gun spun into a dark corner. Now I wasn't acting any more.

I went after him, slammed a hard left to his face, followed with a right to the stomach, then straightened him out with another left. He was a lousy boxer.

The others didn't like it; they closed in and grabbed me.

Knuckles bounced off my jaw as a fist rammed into my back. Two of them ran me backwards and sent me crashing against the wall. My head rang; I was stunned. I fell down and they let me lie. I needed the rest.

To hell with secrecy, I thought. I got to my knees and started crawling toward the corner. The men laughed and shouted, forgetting about being quiet now.

"Crawl, General," one shouted, "Crawl, you lousy spy."

"Hup, two, soldier," another sallied. "By the numbers, crawl."

That was a good one; they roared, slapped each other. Beau Joe had picked himself up and started for me now. Where the hell was that gun?

He grabbed my jacket, hauled me to my feet as I groped for him. My head spun; I must have a concussion, I thought. He jabbed at me, but I leaned on him, and he couldn't get a good swing. The others laughed at him, now, enjoying the farce.

"Watch him, Beau Joe," someone called. "He's liable to wake up, with you shakin' him that way."

Beau Joe stepped back, and aimed a straight right at my chin, but I dropped and headed for the corner again; that was where the gun went. He kicked me again, sent me sprawling into the wall—and my hand fell on the gun.

I rolled over, and Beau Joe yanked me up, spun me around, and stepped back. I stood, slumped in the corner, watching him. He was enjoying it now. He mouthed words silently, grinning in spite of his bleeding mouth. He intended to keep me propped there in the corner and beat me to death. As he came to me, I raised the gun and shot him in the face.

I wished I hadn't; he did a back flip, landed head first, but not before I caught a glimpse of the smashed face. Joe was not beau any more.

I held my hand loosely at my side, waiting for the next comer. The same fellow who had grabbed me before rushed up. He jumped the body and twisted to deliver a skull-crusher. I raised the gun a few inches as he leaped and I fired at his belly. The shot made a hollow whop, as the man's feet left the floor. He smashed into the wall as I sidestepped.

The other three fanned out. It was too dark to see clearly here, and they didn't yet realize what had happened. They thought I had downed the two men with my fists. They were going to jump me together and finish it off.

"Freeze, bunnies!" a voice said from the door. We all looked. A hulking brute stood outlined there, and the gun in his hand was visible.

"I can see you rats," he said. "I'm used to the dark. Don't try nothing." He beckoned a man behind him forward. One of the three in the room edged toward the rear, and the gun coughed, firing through a silencer. The man slammed sideways, and sprawled.

"Come on, Hammer-hand," the big man said. "Let's get out of here." He spat into the room. "These pigeons don't want to play no more."

I recognized the voice of Gaston, the big fellow who had wanted to bury me under the floor. Gros had appointed him my bodyguard, but he was a little late. I had taken a terrible beating. I tucked the gun away clumsily and lurched forward.

"Cripes, Hammer-hand," Gaston said, stepping forward to steady me. "I didn't know them bunnies had got to you; I thought you were stringing them. I was wondering when you was going to make music with that punch."

He paused to stare down at Beau Joe.

"You pushed his mush right in," he said admiringly. "Hey, Touhey, get Hammer-hand's wrap-around, and let's move." He glanced once more around the room.

"So long, bunnies," he said. The two men didn't answer.

CHAPTER NINE

I DON'T remember much about my trip to the Organization's hideout in the country. I recall walking endlessly, and later being carried over Gaston's shoulder. I remember terrific heat, and agonizing pain from my battered face, my half-healed gunshot wounds, and innumerable bruises. And I remember at last a cool room, and a soft bed.

I awoke slowly, dreams blending with memories, none of them pleasant. I lay on my back, propped up on enormous fluffy feather bolsters, with a late afternoon sun lighting the room through partly-drawn drapes over a wide dormer window. For a while I struggled to decide where I was. Gradually I recalled my last conscious thought.

This was the place in the country Gros had been headed for. Gaston had taken his charge seriously, in spite of his own suggestion that I be disposed of and although Miche and Gros were dead.

I moved tentatively, and caught my breath. That hurt, too. My chest, ribs and stomach were one great ache. I pushed the quilt down and tried to examine the damage. Under the edges of a broad tape wrapping, purple bruises showed all around my right side.

Bending my neck had been a mistake; now the bullet wound that Maurice had re-opened with the blackjack began to throb. I was a mess. I didn't risk moving my face; I knew what it must look like.

As a secret-service type, I was a complete bust, I thought. My carefully prepared disguise had fooled no one, except maybe Spider. I had been subjected to more kicks, blows, and threats of death in the few hours I had been in the dictator's realm than in all my previous 42 years, and I had accomplished exactly nothing. I had lost my communicator, and now my slug-gun too; the comforting pressure under my wrist had gone. It wouldn't have helped me much anyway; I was dizzy from the little effort I had just expended.

Maybe I had made some progress, though, in a negative way. I knew that walking in and striking a pose wasn't good enough to get by as the Dictator Bayard, in spite of the face. And I had also learned that the dictator's regime was riddled with subversives and malcontents. Perhaps we could somehow use the latter to our advantage.

If, I thought, I can get back with the information. I thought that over. How would I get back? I had no way of communicating. I was completely on my own now.

Always before I had had the knowledge that in the end I could send out a call for help, and count on rescue within an hour. Richthofen had arranged for a 24-hour monitoring of my communications band, alert for my call. Now that was out. If I was to return to the Imperium, I would have to steal one of the crude shuttles of this world, or better, commandeer one as dictator. I had to get back into the palace, with a correct disguise, or end my days in this nightmare world.

I heard voices approaching outside the room. I closed my eyes as the door opened. I might learn a little by playing possum, if I could get away with it.

The voices were lower now, and I sensed several people coming over to stand by the bed.

"How long has he been asleep?" a new voice asked. Or was it new? It seemed familiar somehow, but I connected it with some other place.

"Doc gave him some shots," someone answered. "We brought him in this time yesterday."

There was a pause. Then the half-familiar voice again. "I don't like his being alive. However—perhaps we can make use of him."

"Gros wanted him alive," another voice said. I recognized Gaston. He sounded sullen. "He had big plans for him."

The other voice grunted. There was a silence for a few moments.

"He's no good to us until the face is healed. Keep him here until I send along further instructions."

I hadn't liked what I heard, but for the present I had no choice but to lie here and try to regain my strength. At least, I was comfortably set up in this huge bed. I drifted off to sleep again.

I awoke with Gaston sitting by the bed, smoking. He sat up when I opened my eyes, crushed out his cigarette in an ashtray on the table, and leaned forward.

"How are you feeling, Hammer-hand?" he said.

"Rested," I said. My voice came out in a faint whisper. I was surprised at its weakness.

"Yeah, them pigeons give you a pretty rough time, Hammer-hand. I don't know why you didn't lay the punch on them sooner.

"I got some chow here for you," Gaston said. He put a tray from the bedside table on his lap and offered me a spoonful of soup. I was hungry; I opened my mouth for it. I never expected to have a gorilla for a nursemaid, I thought.

Gaston was good at his work, though. For the next three days he fed me regularly, changed my bedding, and performed all the duties of a trained nurse with skill, if not with grace. I steadily gained strength, but I was careful to conceal the extent of my progress from Gaston and the others who occasionally came in. I didn't know what might be coming up and I wanted something in reserve.

Gaston told me a lot about the Organization during the next few days. I learned that the group led by Gros and Miche was only one of several such cells; there were hundreds of members, in half a dozen scattered locations in Algeria, each keeping surveillance over some vital installation of the regime. Their ultimate objective was the overthrow of Bayard's rule, enabling them to get a share in the loot.

Each group had two leaders, all of whom reported to the Big Boss, a stranger about whom Gaston knew little. He appeared irregularly, and no one knew his name or where he had his headquarters. I sensed that Gaston didn't like him.

On the third day I asked Gaston to help me get up and walk a bit. I faked extreme weakness, but was pleased to discover that I was feeling better than I had hoped. After Gaston helped me back into bed and left the room, I got up again, and practiced walking. It made me dizzy and nauseous but I leaned on the bedpost and waited for my stomach to settle down, and went on. I stayed on my feet for fifteen minutes, and slept soundly afterwards. Thereafter, whenever I awoke, day or night, I rose and walked, jumping back into bed when I heard footsteps approaching.

When Gaston insisted on walking me after that, I continued to feign all the symptoms I had felt the first time. The doctor was called back once, but he assured me that my reactions were quite normal, and that I could not expect to show much improvement for another week, considering the amount of blood I had lost. This suited me perfectly. I needed time to learn more.

I tried to pump Gaston about my disguise, subtly; I didn't want to put him on his guard, or give him any inkling of what I had in mind. But I was too subtle; Gaston avoided the subject.

I searched for my clothes, but the closet was locked and I couldn't risk forcing the door.

A week after my arrival, I allowed myself enough improvement to permit a walk through the house, and down into a pleasant garden behind it. The layout of the house was simple. From the garden I had seen no signs of guards. It looked as though I could walk out any time, but I restrained the impulse.

By the time ten days had passed, I was getting very restless. I couldn't fake my role of invalid much longer without arousing suspicion. The inactivity was getting on my nerves; I had spent the night lying awake, thinking, and getting up occasionally to walk up and down the room. By dawn, I had succeeded in fatiguing myself, but I hadn't slept at all.

I had to be doing something. I got out my canes, and reconnoitered the house after Gaston had taken away my breakfast tray. From the upstairs windows I had a wide view of the surrounding country. The front of the house faced a paved highway, in good repair. I assumed it was a main route into Algiers. Behind the house, tilled fields stretched a quarter of a mile to a row of trees. Perhaps there was a river there. There were no other houses near.

I thought about leaving. It looked to me as though my best bet would be to go over the wall after dark and head for the cover of the trees. I had the impression that the line of trees and the road converged to the west, so perhaps I could regain the road at a distance from the house, and follow it into the city. I went back to my room to wait.

It was almost dinnertime when I heard someone approaching my door. I was lying down, so I stayed where I was and waited. Gaston entered with the doctor. The doctor was pale, and perspiring heavily. He avoided my eyes as he drew out a chair, sat down and started his examination. He said nothing to me, ignoring the questions I asked him. I gave up and lay silently while he prodded and poked. After a while he rose suddenly, packed up his kit, and walked out.

"What's the matter with the doc, Gaston?" I asked.

"He's got something on his mind," Gaston said. Even Gaston seemed subdued. Something was up; something that worried me.

"Come on, Gaston," I said. "What's going on?"

At first I thought he wasn't going to answer me.

"They're going to do like you wanted," he said. "They're getting ready to put you in for Bayard."

"That's fine," I said. That was what I had come here for. This way was as good as any. But there was something about it.

"Why all the secrecy?" I asked. "Why doesn't the Big Boss show himself? I'd like to talk to him."

Gaston hesitated. I had the feeling he wanted to say more, but couldn't.

"They got a few details to fix yet," he said. He didn't look at me. I let it go at that.

After Gaston left the room, I went out into the hall. Through the open back windows I heard the sound of conversation. I moved over to eavesdrop.

There were three men, strolling out into the garden with their backs to me. One was the doctor; I didn't recognize the other two. I wished I could see their faces.

"It was not for this I was trained," the doctor was saying. He waved his hands in an agitated way. "I'm not a butcher, to cut up a side of mutton for you."

I couldn't make out the reply.

I went down to the landing and listened. All was quiet. I descended to the hall on the ground floor, listened again. Somewhere a clock was ticking.

I went into the main dining room; the table was set for three, but no food was in sight. I tried the other dining room; nothing. I went across and eased the parlor door open. There was no one there; it looked as unused as ever.

I passed the door I had found locked once before and noticed light under it. I stepped back and tried it. It was probably a broom closet, I thought as I turned the knob. It opened.

I stood staring. There was a padded white table in the center of the room. At one end stood two flood-lamps on tall tripods. Glittering instruments were laid out on a small table. On a stand beside the operating table lay scalpels, sutures, heavy curved needles. There was a finely made saw, like a big hacksaw, and heavy snippers. On the floor beneath the table was a large galvanized steel wash tub.

I didn't understand this; I turned to the door—and heard footsteps approaching.

I looked around, saw a door, jumped to it and jerked it open. When the two men entered the room, I was standing rigid in the darkness of the storeroom, with the door open half an inch.

The floodlights flicked on, then off again. There was a rattle of metal against metal.

"Layoff that," a nasal voice said. "This is all set. I checked it over myself."

"They're nuts," Nasal-voice said. "Why don't they wait until morning, when they got plenty sunlight for this? No, they gotta work under the lights."

"I don't get this deal," a thin voice said. "I didn't get what was supposed to be wrong with this guy's legs, they got to take them off. How come if he's—"

"You ain't clued in, are you, Mac?" Nasal-voice said harshly. "This is a big deal; they're going to ring this mug in when they knock off the Old Man."

"Yeah, that's what I mean," Thin-voice cut in. "So what's the idea they take off the legs?"

"You don't know much, do you, small-timer?" Nasal voice said. "Well, listen; I got news for you." There was a pause.

"Bayard's got no pins, from the knees down." Nasal spoke in a hushed tone. "You didn't know that, did you? That's why you never seen him walking around on the video; he's always sitting back of a desk.

"There ain't very many people know about that," he added. "Keep it to yourself."

"Cripes," Thin-voice said. His voice was thinner than ever. "Got no legs?"

"That's right. I was with him a year before the landing. I was in his outfit when he got it. Machine gun slug, through both knees. Now forget about it. But maybe now you get the set-up.

"Cripes," Thin-voice said. "Where did they get a guy crazy enough to go into a deal like this?"

"How do I know," the other said. He sounded as though he regretted having told the secret. "These revolutionist types is all nuts anyway."

I stood there feeling sick. My legs tingled. I knew now why nobody mistook me for the dictator, as I walked into a room; and why Spider had been taken in, when he saw me sitting.

I was leaving now. Not tomorrow, not tonight; now. I had no gun, no papers, no map, no plans, but I was leaving.

It was almost dark; I went to the back of the house. Through a window I could see the men in the garden standing under a small cherry tree in the gloom, still talking. I found a door, and examined it in the failing light. It was the type that opens in two sections. The upper one was locked, but the lower half swung silently open—below the line of vision of the men outside. I bent over and stepped through.

A short path led off to the drive beside the house; I ignored it and crept along beside the wall, through weed grown flowerbeds.

I turned to start out across the plowed field and a dark form rose up before me. I recoiled, my wrist twitching in a gesture that had become automatic; but no slug-gun snapped into my hand. I was unarmed, weak, and shaken, and the man loomed over me, hulking.

"Let's go, Hammer-hand," he whispered. It was Gaston.

"I'm leaving, Gaston," I said. "Just don't try to stop me."

Vague ideas of a bluff were in my mind. After all, he called me Hammer-hand.

He came after me. "Hold it down to a roar," he said. "I wondered when you was going to make your break. You been getting pretty restless these last few days."

"Yeah," I said. "Who wouldn't?" I was just stalling; I had no plan.

"You got more nerve than me, Hammer-hand," Gaston said. "I would of took off a week ago. You must of wanted to get a look at the Big Boss real bad to stick as long as you did."

"I saw enough today," I said. "I don't want to see any more."

"Do you make him?" Gaston asked. He sounded interested.

"No," I said. "I didn't see his face. But I've lost my curiosity."

Gaston laughed. "OK, chief," he said. He handed me a soiled card, with something scribbled on it. "Maybe this will do you some good. It's the Big Boss's address out of town. I swiped it; it was all I could find. Now let's blowout of here."

I stuck the card in my pocket. I was a little confused.

"Wait a minute, Gaston; you mean you're helping me get away?"

"Gros said I was supposed to keep an eye on you, look out you didn't have no accident," Gaston said. "I always done all right doing what my brother told me; I don't see no reason to stop now just because they killed him."

"Your brother," I said.

"Gros was my brother," Gaston said. "I ain't smart like Gros, but he always took care of me. I always done what he said. He told me to look out for you, Hammer-hand."

"What about them?" I asked, nodding toward the house. "They won't like it when they find us both missing."

Gaston spat. "To hell with them monkeys," he said. "They gimme the willies."

I was beginning to feel jolly all of a sudden, by reaction:

"Listen, Gaston; can you go back in there and get the clothes I had on when I got here?"

Gaston fumbled in the dark at a sack slung over his shoulder. "I thought you might want that suit, Hammer-hand," he said. "You was real particular about that with Miche." He handed me a bundle. I knew the feel of it. It was the uniform.

"Gaston," I said. "You're a wonder. I don't suppose you brought along the little gimmick I had on my wrist?"

"I think I stuck it in the pocket," he said. "Somebody swiped the fancy gloves you had in the belt, though. I'm sorry about the gloves."

I fumbled over the blouse, and felt the lump in the pocket. With that slug-gun in my hand I was ready to lick the world.

"That's OK about the gloves, Gaston," I said. I strapped the clip to my wrist and tucked the gun away. I pulled off the old coat I wore and slipped the blouse on. This was more like it.

I looked at the house. All was peaceful. It was dark enough now that we wouldn't be seen crossing the field. It was time to go.

"Come on," I said. I took a sight on a bright star and struck out across the soft ground.

In fifty steps the house was completely lost to view. The wall and high foliage obscured the lights on the first floor; upstairs the house was in darkness. I kept the star before me and stumbled on. I never knew how hard it was to walk in a plowed field in the dark.

It was fifteen minutes before I made out a deeper darkness against the faintly lighter sky ahead. That would be the line of trees along the river; I was still assuming there was a river.

Then we were among the trees, feeling our way slowly. The ground sloped and the next moment I was sliding down a muddy bank into shallow water.

"Yes," I said, "it's a river all right." I scrambled out, and stood peering toward the west. I could see nothing. If we had to pick our way through trees all night, without a moon, we wouldn't be a mile away by dawn.

"Which way does this river flow, Gaston?" I asked.

"That way," he said. "To Algiers—into the city."

"Can you swim?" I asked.

"Sure," Gaston replied. "I can swim good."

"OK," I said. "Strip and make a bundle of your clothes. Put whatever you don't want to get wet in the middle; strap the bundle to your shoulders with your belt."

We grunted and fumbled in the darkness.

I finished my packing and stepped down into the water. It was warm weather; that was a break. I still had the slug-gun on my wrist. I wanted it close to me.

I stepped out into the stream, pushed off as the bottom shelved. I paddled a few strokes to get clear of the reeds growing near the shore. All around was inky blackness, with only the brilliant stars overhead to relieve the emptiness.

"OK, Gaston?" I called.

I heard him splashing quietly.

"Sure," he said.

"Let's go out a little farther and then take it easy," I said. "Let the river do the work."

CHAPTER TEN

THE CURRENT was gentle. Far across the river I saw a tiny light now. We drifted slowly past it. I moved my hands just enough to keep my nose above water. The surface was calm. I yawned; I could have slept tonight, I thought, remembering the sleepless hours of the night before. But it would be a long time between beds for me.

I saw a glinting reflection on a ripple ahead, and glanced back. There were lights on in the second story of the house we had left.

I called to Gaston, pointing out the lights.

"Yeah," he said. "I been watching them. I don't think we got nothing to worry about."

They could follow our trail to the water's edge easily enough, I knew, with nothing more than a flashlight. As if in response to my thought, a tiny gleam appeared at ground level, wavering, blinking as the trees passed between us. It moved, bobbing toward the river. I watched until it emerged from the trees. I saw the yellow gleam dancing across the water where we had started. Other lights were following now, two, three.

The whole household must have joined the chase. They must be expecting to find me huddled on the ground nearby, exhausted, ready for the table they had prepared for me in the presence of my enemies.

The lights fanned out, moving along the shore. I saw that we were safely ahead of them.

"Gaston," I said, "have they got a boat back there?"

"Nah," he replied. "We're in the clear."

The little lights were pitiful, bobbing along the shore, falling behind.

We floated along then in silence for an hour or more. It was still, almost restful. Only a gentle fluttering of the hands was required to keep our heads above water.

Suddenly lights flashed ahead, over the river.

"Cripes," Gaston hissed, backing water. "I forgot about the Salan bridge. Them bunnies is on there waitin' for us."

I could see the bridge, now, as the lights flashed across the pilings. It was about a hundred yards ahead.

"Head for the far shore, Gaston," I said. "Fast and quiet."

I couldn't risk the splash of a crawl stroke, so I dog-paddled frantically, my hands under the surface. They would have had us neatly, if they hadn't shown the lights when they did, I thought. They couldn't see us without them, though, so it was just a chance they had to take. They must have estimated the speed of the river's flow, and tried to pinpoint us. They didn't miss by much; in fact, they might not have missed at all. I concentrated on putting every ounce of energy into my strokes. My knees hit mud, and reeds brushed my face. I rolled over and sat up, breathing hard. Gaston floundered a few feet away.

"Here," I hissed. "Keep it quiet."

The light on the bridge blinked out suddenly. I wondered what they'd do next. If they headed along the banks, flashing lights, we'd have to take to the water again; and if one man stayed on the bridge, and flashed his light down just about the right moment—

"Let's get going," I said.

I started up the slope, crouching low. The lights appeared again, down at the water's edge now, flashing on the tall grass and cattails. Another appeared on the opposite bank. I stopped to listen. Feet made sloshing sounds in the mud, a hundred feet away. Good; that would cover our noise. My wet shoes dangled by the strings, thumping my chest.

The ground was firmer now, the grass not so tall. I stopped again, Gaston right behind me, looking back. They'd find our tracks any minute. We had no time to waste. The bundle of clothing was a nuisance, but we couldn't stop to dress now.

"Come on," I whispered, and broke into a run.

Fifty feet from the top we dropped and started crawling. I didn't want to be seen in silhouette against the sky as we topped the rise.

We pulled ourselves along, puffing and grunting. Crawling is hard work for a grown man. Just over the top we paused to look over the situation. The road leading to the bridge wound away toward a distant glow in the sky.

"That's an army supply depot out that way," Gaston said. "No town."

I raised up to look back toward the river. Two lights bobbed together, then started slowly away from the water's edge. I heard a faint shout.

"They've spotted the trail," I said. I jumped up and ran down the slope, trying to breathe deep, in for four strides, out for four. A man could run for a long time if he didn't get winded. Stones bruised my bare feet.

I angled over toward the highway, with some idea of making better time. Gaston was beside me.

"Nix," he said, puffing hard. "Them bunnies got a machine."

For a moment I didn't know what he meant; then I heard the sound of an engine starting up, and headlights lanced into the darkness, beams aimed at the distant tree-tops as the car headed up the slope of the approach to the bridge from the other side. We had only a few seconds before the car would slant down on this side, and illuminate the road and a wide strip on either side; we'd be spotlighted.

Ahead, I saw a fence, just a glint from a wire. That finished it; we were stopped. I slid to a halt. Then I saw that the fence lined a crossroad, joining the road we were paralleling twenty feet away. Maybe a culvert...I dived for shelter.

A corrugated steel pipe eighteen inches in diameter ran beside the main road where the other joined it. I scrambled over pebbles and twigs and into the mouth. The sounds I made echoed hollowly inside. I kept going to the far end, Gaston wheezing behind me. I stopped and looked over my shoulder. Gaston had backed in and lay a few feet inside his end. The glow of the headlights gave me a glimpse of a heavy automatic in his hand.

"Good boy," I hissed. "Don't shoot unless you have to."

The lights of the car flickered over trees, highlighting rocks. Through the open end of the pipe I saw a rabbit sitting up in the glare, a few feet away. He turned and bounded off.

The car came slowly along, passed, moved on down the road. I breathed a little easier.

I was on the point of turning to say something to Gaston when a small stone rolled down into the ditch before me. I stiffened. A faint scuff of shoes on gravel, another stone dislodged—and then a flashlight beam darted across the gully, played on the grass opposite, came to rest on the open end of the drain pipe. I held my breath. Then the steps came nearer, and the light probed, found my shoulder. There was a frozen instant of silence, then the sharp slap of the slug-gun hitting my palm. I caught a glimpse of the car a hundred feet away now, still edging along, heard a sharp intake of breath as the man with the light readied a shout. I pointed the gun to the right of the flash and the recoil slammed my arm back. The flashlight skidded across the rocky ground and went out as the man's body crashed heavily and lay still. I groped for the man's feet, hauled him back toward the pipe.

"Gaston," I whispered. The sound was hollow in the dark tunnel. "Give me a hand." I pulled at the feet. I was glad it wasn't the doctor; he wouldn't have fitted.

I crawled out of the pipe and Gaston came up beside me.

"After the car," I said. I had what I hoped was an idea. I was tired of being chased; the hunted would become the hunter.

I headed up the ditch at a trot, head down, Gaston at my heels. The car had stopped a hundred yards away. I counted three flashlights moving in the edge of the field.

"Close enough," I hissed. "Let's split up now. I'll cross the road and come up the other side. There's only one man over there. You get up in the tall grass and sneak in as close to the car as you can. Watch me and take your cue."

I darted across the road, a grotesque figure, naked, my bundle dangling by its strap from my shoulder. The car's headlights were still on. No one could see us from beyond them, looking into the glare. I dropped down into the ditch, wincing as sharp sticks jabbed my bare feet. The man on my side was casting about in wide circles, fifty feet from the road. A cricket sawed away insistently.

The car started backing, swung to one side of the road, then went forward; the driver was in the car, all right, he was turning around. They must have come up the road to cut us off, planning to move back to the river, searching foot by foot until they flushed us. No one seemed to have missed the man who now lay quietly in the steel pipe.

The car swung around and moved along at a snail's pace, headlights flooding the road I had just crossed. I dropped down to the bottom of the ditch as the lights passed over me. The car came on, and stopped just above me. I could see the driver, staring out through the windshield. He leaned forward, peering. I wondered if he was looking for the man who had been coming along on foot, checking the ditch; he'd be a long time seeing him from here.

He opened the door, stepped out, one foot on the running board. The car was long and top-heavy with flaring fenders. Dust roiled and gnats danced in the beams from the great bowl-shaped headlights.

I picked up a heavy stone, rose silently to hands and knees, and crept up out of the ditch. The chauffeur stood with a hand on the top of the door, looking over it. I came up behind him and hit him as hard as I could on the top of the head, he folded into the seat. I shoved him over, jumped in, and closed the door. It was hard to get the coat off him in the dark, while trying to stay down behind the door, but I managed it. I put it on and sat up. There was no alarm. The three flashlights continued to bob around in the fields. The engine was running quietly.

I looked over the controls. The steering wheel was in the center, and there were three pedals on the floor. I let the center pedal in; the car moved off slowly. I steered to the right side of the road, crept along the edge. Gaston must be about here, I thought. I stared out into the darkness; I could see practically nothing.

I eased to a stop. The flashlight nearest me swung back and forth, moving toward the bridge. I reached out to the dash, pushed in a lever that projected from it. The headlights died.

I could see better now. The flashlights to my right stopped moving, turned toward me. I waved cheerfully. I didn't think they could make out my face in the dim beam at that distance. One of the lights seemed satisfied, resumed its search; the other hesitated, flashing over the car.

There was a shout then, and I saw Gaston up and running toward me. The flashlights converged on him as he leaped across the ditch ahead, coming into the road. The lights came bounding toward him and someone was yelling. Gaston stopped, whirled toward the nearest light, aiming the pistol. There was a sharp sound. Both lights on his side dropped. Not bad shooting for a .45, I thought. I jerked open the door and Gaston jumped in beside me. Behind there was a faint shout from the remaining man on the other side of the road, and the crack of a gun. The slug made a solid thunk as it hit the heavy steel of the car. I floorboarded the center and left pedals; the car jumped ahead, then coasted. Another slug starred the glass beside me, scattering glass chips in my hair. I let my foot off, tried again. The car surged forward. I flipped the lights on. The car shifted up, tires squealing. Ahead, a figure stumbled down into the ditch, scrambled up the other side into the road, waving its arms. I saw the open mouth in the taut white face for an instant in the flare of the lights before it was slammed down out of sight, with a shock that bounced us in our seats.

The bridge loomed ahead, narrow and highly arched. We took it wide open, crushed down in the seat as we mounted the slope, floating as we dropped on the other side. The road curved off to the left, tall trees lining it. The tires howled as we rounded the turn and hit the straightaway.

"This is great, Hammer-hand," Gaston shouted. "I never rode in one of these here machines before."

"Neither did I," I yelled back.

CHAPTER ELEVEN

THE NIGHT was black, with no moon. My next problem was to get into the walled town. The road led along the river's edge into the heart of the city, according to Gaston. The dictator's stronghold lay at the edge of the city north of the highway we were on. He had fortified the area, enclosing shops and houses within an encircling wall like a medieval town, creating a self-sufficient community to support the castle and its occupants, easily patrolled and policed. It was no defense against an army, but practical as a safeguard against assassins and rioters.

"That's us," I said aloud. "Assassins and rioters."

"Sure, chief," Gaston said.

There was a glow in the sky ahead. From the road only a few scattered lights were visible. The countryside seemed almost unpopulated.

Twenty minutes of driving brought us to the bombed-out edge of the city. The rubble stretched ahead, with here and there a shack or a tiny patch of garden. To the right the mass of the castle loomed up, faintly visible in the glow from the streets below it, unseen behind the wall. To the original massive old country house, Bayard had added rambling outbuildings, great mismatched wings, and the squat tower.

I pulled over, cut the headlights. Gaston and I looked silently at the lights in the tower. He lit a cigarette.

"How are we going to get in there, Gaston?" I said. "How do we get over the wall?"

Gaston stared at the walls, thinking. "Listen, Hammer-hand," he said. "You wait here, while I check around a little. I'm pretty good at casing a layout, and I know this one from the inside; I'll find a spot if there is one. Keep an eye peeled for the street gangs."

I sat and waited. I rolled up the windows and locked the doors. I couldn't see any signs of life about the broken walls around me. Somewhere a cat yowled.

I checked my clothes over. Both lapels were missing; the tiny set was still clipped to my belt, but without speaker or mike, it was useless. I ran my tongue over the tooth with the cyanide sealed in it. I might need it yet.

The door rattled. I had dozed off. Gaston's face pressed against the glass. I unlocked it and he slid in beside me.

"OK, Hammer-hand," he said. "Think I got us a spot. We go along the edge of the drainage ditch over there to where it goes under the wall. Then we got to get down inside it and ease under the guard tower. It comes out in the clear on the other side."

I got out and followed Gaston over broken stones to the ditch. It was almost a creek, and the smell of it was terrible.

Gaston led me along its edge for a hundred yards, until the wall hung over us just beyond the circle of light from the guard tower. I could see a fellow with a burp gun leaning against a post on top of the tower, looking down onto the street inside the wall. There were two large floodlights beside him, unlit.

Gaston leaned close to my ear. "It kind of stinks," he said, "but the wall is pretty rough, so I think we can make it OK."

He slid over the edge, found a foothold, and disappeared. I slid down after him, groping with my foot for a ledge. The wall was crudely laid, with plenty of cracks and projecting stones, but slimy with moss. I groped along, one precarious foot at a time. We passed the place where the light gleamed on the black water below, hugging the shadow. Then we were under the wall, which arched massively over us. The sound of trickling water was louder here.

I tried to see what was going on ahead. Gaston had stopped and was descending. I could barely make out his figure, knee-deep in the malodorous stream. I moved closer. Then I saw the grating. It was made of iron bars, and completely blocked the passage.

I climbed over to the grating, leaned against the rusty iron to ease my arms. The defense system didn't have quite the hole in it we thought it had. Gaston moved around below me, reaching under the surface to try to find a bottom edge. Maybe we could duck under the barrier.

Suddenly I felt myself slipping.

Below me, Gaston hissed a curse, scrabbled upward. My grip was firm, I realized in an instant; it was the grating that was slipping. It dropped another eight inches with a muffled scraping and clank, then stopped. The rusty metal had given under our weight. The corroded ends of the bars had broken off at the left side. There wasn't room to pass, but maybe we could force it a little further.

Gaston braced himself against the wall and heaved. I got into position beside him and added my weight. The frame shifted a little, then stuck.

"Gaston," I said. "Maybe I can get under it now, and heave from the other side." Gaston moved back, and I let myself down into the reeking water. I worked an arm through, then dropped down waist deep, chest deep, pushing.

The rough metal scraped my face, caught at my clothing; but I was through.

I crawled back up, dripping, and rested. From the darkness behind Gaston I heard a meshing of oiled metal parts and then the cavern echoed with the thunder of machine gun fire. In the flashing light I saw Gaston stiffen against the grating and fall. He hung by one hand, caught in the grating. There were shouts, and men dropped onto the stone coping at the culvert mouth. Gaston jerked, fumbled his pistol from his blouse.

"Gaston," I said. "Quick, under the bars…" I was helpless. I knew he was too big.

A man appeared, clinging to the coping with one hand, climbing down to enter the dark opening. He flashed a light at us and Gaston, still dangling by the left hand, fired. The man fell over into the stream with a tremendous splash.

Gaston gasped. "That's…all…" The gun fell from his hand into the black water.

I moved fast now, from one handhold to the next, slipping and clutching, but not quite falling somehow. I managed to get a look back as I reached the open air. Two men were tugging at the body wedged in the opening. Even in death, Gaston guarded my retreat.

I came up over the side, and flattened against the wall, slug-gun in my hand; the street was empty. They must have thought they had us trapped; this side was deserted. I was directly under the tower. I eased out a few feet, and craned my neck; a shadow moved at the top of the tower. There was still one man on duty there. He must have heard the grating fall and called for reinforcements.

I looked down the street ahead. I recognized the Street of the Olive Trees, the same one I had come through on my way out with Gros, ten days earlier. It slanted down, curving to the right. That was where I had to go, into the naked street, under the guns. I liked it here in the shadow of the tower, but I couldn't stay. I leaped forward, running for my life. The searchlight snapped on, swung, found me, burning my leaping shadow against dusty walls and the loose-cobbled street. Instinct told me to leap aside. As I did, the gun clattered and slugs whined off the stones to my left. I was out of the light now, and dashing for the protection of the curving wall ahead. The light was still groping as I rounded the turn. No lights came on above me; I ran in utter silence. The dwellers in these scarred tenements had learned to sit silent behind barred windows when guns talked in the narrow streets.

I passed the spot where Gros had died, dashed on. In the distance a whistle blew again and again. A shot rang out, kicking up dust ahead. I kept going.

I heard running feet behind me now. I scanned the shabby stalls ahead, empty and dark, trying to find the one we had used the day we left the palace, where the old woman huddled over her table of clay ware. It had been tiny, with a ragged gray awning sagging over the front and broken pots scattered before it.

I almost passed it, caught myself, skidded, and dived for the back. I fought the stiff tarpaulin, found the opening and squeezed through.

I panted in complete darkness now. Outside, I heard voices as the men shouted to each other, searching. I had a moment's respite; they didn't know this entry.

I looked at my watch. Things happened fast in this war world; it was not yet half past nine. I had left the house at seven. I had killed three men in those two hours, and a man had died for me. I thought how easily a man slips back to his ancient role as nature's most deadly hunter.

I felt the fatigue suddenly. I yawned, sat on the floor. I had an impulse to lie back and go to sleep, but instead I got up and began feeling my way toward the passage. I wasn't finished yet; I was in the palace, unwounded, armed. I had all I had any right to hope for—a fighting chance.

I was no longer the eager neophyte, ignorant of the realities; I came now, steeled by necessity, a hardened fighter, a practical killer. I was armed and I was desperate, and I bore the scars of combat. I did not intend to fail.

Half an hour later, I eased a door open and looked down the length of the same hall into which the shuttle had pitched me headlong two weeks before. It hadn't changed. I stepped into the hall, tried the first door. It opened, and I saw that it was a bedroom. I went in, and by the faint light shining through the curtains from below, looked over a wide bed, a large desk against the far wall, a closet door, an easy chair, and through a partly open door, a roomy bathroom to the right. I closed the door behind me, and crossed to the windows. There were steel shutters, painted light green to match the walls, folded back behind the draperies. I closed them, then went to the desk and flipped on the lamp. I had had enough of groping through the dark for one night.

The room was very handsome, spacious, with a deep pile grey-green rug and a pair of bold watercolors on the wall. Suddenly I was aware of my own reek. The clothes seemed to crawl on my back. I had lain in mud, waded a sewer, crept through ancient dust. Without considering further, I pulled the encrusted tunic off, tossed my clothes in a heap by the door, and headed for the bath.

I took half an hour soaping myself, and then climbed out and got my uniform. I had nothing else to put on, and I wouldn't wear it as it was. I soaped it up, rinsed it out, and draped it over the side of the tub. There was a vast white bathrobe behind the door, and I wrapped myself in it and went back into the bedroom.

The thought penetrated to my dulled mind that I was behaving dangerously. I tried again to shake myself alert. But alarm wouldn't come. I felt perfectly safe, secure, comfortable. This won't do, I thought; I'm going to go to sleep on my feet. I yawned again.

I sat down in the chair opposite the door, and prepared to wait it out. I got up, as an after-thought, and turned the light out. I don't remember sitting down again.

CHAPTER TWELVE

I DREAMT I was at the seashore, and the sun reflected from the glassy water. It flashed in my eyes, and I turned away. I twisted in the chair, opened my eyes. My head was thick.

I stared at the pale green walls of the room, across the grey-green rug. It was silent in the room and I didn't move. The door stood open.

I remembered turning the light off, nothing more. Someone had turned it on; someone had opened the door. I had come as a killer in the night; and someone had found me here sleeping, betrayed by my own exhaustion.

I sat up, and in that instant realized I was not alone. I turned my head, and looked at the man who sat quietly in the chair on my left, leaning back with his legs thrust out stiffly before him, his hands lightly gripping the arms of a rosewood chair upholstered in black leather. He smiled, and leaned forward. It was like looking into a mirror.

I didn't move. I stared at him. His face was thinner than mine, more lined. The skin was burned dark, the hair bleached lighter by the African sun; but it was me I looked at. Not a twin, not a double, not a clever actor; it was myself, sitting in a chair, looking at me.

"You have been sleeping soundly," he said. I thought of hearing my voice on a tape recorder, except this voice spoke in flawless French.

I moved my hand slightly; my gun was still there, and the man I had come to kill sat not ten feet away, alone, unprotected. But I didn't move. I wasn't ready, not yet. Maybe not ever.

"Are you rested enough," he said, "or will you sleep longer before we talk?"

"I'm rested," I said.

"I do not know how you came here," he said, "but that you are here is enough. I did not know what gift the tide of fortune would bring to me, but there could be no finer thing than this—a brother."

I didn't know what I had expected the Dictator Bayard to be—a sullen ruffian, a wild-eyed megalomaniac, a sly-eyed schemer. But I had not expected a breathing image of myself, with a warm smile, and a poetic manner of speech, a man who called me brother.

He looked at me with an expression of intense interest.

"You speak excellent French, but with an English accent," he said. "Or is it perhaps American?" He smiled. "You must forgive my curiosity. Linguistics, accents, they are a hobby of mine and, in your case, I am doubly intrigued."

"American," I said.

"Amazing," he said. "I might have been born an American myself...but that is a long dull tale to tell another time."

No need, I thought. My father told it to me often, when I was a boy.

He went on, his voice intense, but gentle, friendly.

"They told me, when I returned to Algiers ten days ago, that a man resembling myself had been seen here in the apartment. There were two men found in my study, quite dead. There was a great deal of excitement, a garbled report. But I was struck by the talk of a man who looked like me. I wanted to see him, talk to him; I have been so very much alone here. It was a thing that caught my imagination. Of course, I did not know what brought this man here; they even talked of danger..." He spread his hands in a Gaelic gesture.

"But when I came into this room and found you here, sleeping, I knew at once that you could not have come but in friendship. I was touched, my friend, to see that you came here on your own, entrusting yourself to my hands."

I couldn't say anything. I didn't try.

"When I lit the lamp and saw your face, I knew at once that this was more than some shallow impersonation; I saw my own face there, not so worn by war as my own, the lines not so deeply etched. But there was the call of blood to blood; I knew you for my brother."

I licked my lips, swallowed. He leaned forward, placed his hand over mine, gripped it hard, then leaned back in his chair with a sigh.

"Forgive me again, brother. I fall easily into oratory, I fear; a habit I should do well to break. There is time enough for plans later. But now, will you tell me of yourself? I know you have in you the blood of the Bayards."

"Yes, my name is Bayard."

"You must have wanted very much to come to me, to have made your way here alone and unarmed. No one has ever passed the wall before, without an escort and many papers."

I couldn't sit here silent, but neither could I tell this man anything of my real purpose in coming. I reminded myself of the treatment the Imperial ambassadors had received at his hands, of all that Bale had told me that first morning in the meeting with Bernadette. But I saw nothing here of the ruthless tyrant I expected. Instead, I found myself responding to his spontaneous welcome.

I had to tell him something. My years of diplomatic experience came to my assistance once again. I found myself lying smoothly.

"You're right in thinking I can help you, Brion," I said. I was startled to hear myself calling him by his first name so easily, but it seemed the natural thing to do.

"But you're wrong in assuming that your state is the only surviving center of civilization. There is another, a strong, dynamic, and friendly power, which would like to establish amicable relations with you. I am the emissary of that government."

"But why did you not come to me openly? The course you chose, while daring, was of extreme danger; but it must be that you were aware of the treachery all about me, and feared that my enemies would keep you from me."

He seemed so eager to understand that he supplied most of his own answers. This seemed an opportune moment to broach the subject of Bale's two agents who had carried full diplomatic credentials, and who had been subjected to beating, torture, and death. It was a contradiction in the dictator's character I wanted to shed a little light on.

"I recall that two men sent to you a year ago were not well received," I said. "I was unsure of my reception. I wanted to see you privately, face to face."

Bayard's face tensed. "Two men?" he said. "I have heard nothing of ambassadors."

"They were met first by a Colonel-General Yang," I said, "and afterward were interviewed by you personally."

Bayard's face went red. "There is a dog of a broken officer who leads a crew of cut-throats in raids on what pitiful commerce I have been able to encourage. His name is Yang.

If he has molested a legation sent to me from your country, I promise you his head."

"It was said that you yourself shot one of them," I said., pressing the point.

Bayard gripped the arm of the chair, his eyes on my face.

"I swear to you by the honor of the House of Bayard that I have never heard until this moment of your Embassy, and that no harm came to them through any act of mine."

I believed him. I was starting to wonder about a lot of things. He seemed sincere in welcoming the idea of an alliance with a civilized power. And yet, I myself had seen the carnage done by his raiders at the palace, and the atom bomb they had tried to detonate there.

"Very well," I said. "On behalf of my government, I accept your statement; but if we treaty with you now, what assurance will be given to us that there will be no repetition of the bombing raids?"

"Bombing raids!" He stared at me. There was a silence. "Thank God you came to me by night, in secret," he said. "It is plain to me now that control of affairs has slipped from me farther even than I had feared."

"There have been seven raids, four of them accompanied by atomic bombs, in the past year," I said. "The most recent was less than one month ago."

His voice was deadly now. "By my order, every gram of fissionable material known to me to exist was dumped into the sea on the day that I established this state. That there were traitors in my service, I knew; but that there were madmen who would begin the horror again, I did not suspect."

He turned and stared across the room at a painting of sunlight shining through leaves onto a weathered wall. "I fought them when they burned the libraries, melted down the Cellini altar pieces, trampled the Mona Lisa in the ruins of the

Louvre. I could save only a fragment here, a remnant there, always telling myself that it was not too late. But the years passed and they have brought no change.

"There has been an end to industry, farming, family life. Even with the plenty that lies about us for the taking, men fight over three things: gold, liquor, and women.

"I have tried to arouse a spirit of rebuilding against the day when even the broken storehouses run dry; but it's useless. Only my rigid martial rule holds them in check.

"I will confess. I had lost hope. There was too much decay all around me. In my own house, among my closest advisors, I heard nothing but talk of armament, expeditionary forces, domination, renewed war against the ruins outside our little island of order. Empty war, meaningless overlordship of dead nations. They hoped to spend our slender resources in stamping out whatever traces might remain of human achievement, unless it bowed to our supremacy."

When he looked at me I thought of the expression, "Blazing eyes."

"Now my hope springs up renewed," he said. "With a brother at my side, we will prevail."

I thought about it. The Imperium had given me full powers. I might as well use them.

"I think I can assure you," I said, "that the worst is over. My government has resources; you may ask for whatever you need—men, supplies, equipment. We ask only one thing of you—friendship and justice between us."

He leaned back, closed his eyes. "The long night is over," he said.

There were still major points to be covered, but I felt sure that Bayard had been grossly misrepresented to me, and to the Imperial government. I wondered how Imperial Intelligence had been so completely taken in and why. Bale had spoken of having a team of his best men here, sending a stream of data back to him.

There was also the problem of my transportation back to the Zero Zero world of the Imperium. Bayard hadn't mentioned the MC shuttles. In fact, thinking over what he had said, he talked as though they didn't exist. Perhaps he was holding out on me, in spite of his apparent candor.

Bayard opened his eyes. "There has been enough of gravity for now," he said. "I think that a little rejoicing between us would be appropriate. I wonder if you share my liking for an impromptu feast on such an occasion?"

"I love to eat in the middle of the night," I said, "especially when I've missed my dinner."

"You are a true Bayard," he said. He reached to the table beside me and pressed a button. He leaned back and placed his fingertips together.

"And so now we must think about the menu." He pursed his lips, looking thoughtful. "Tonight, permit me to select the menu," he said. "We will see if our tastes are as similar as ourselves."

"Fine," I said.

There was a tap at the door. At Brion's call, it opened and a sour-faced fiftyish little man came in. He saw me, started; then his face blanked. He crossed to the dictator's chair, drew himself up, and said, "I came as quick as I could, Major."

"Fine, fine, Luc," he said. "At ease. My brother and I are hungry. We have a very special hunger, and I want you, Luc, to see to it that our dinner does the kitchen credit."

Luc glanced at me from the corner of his eye. "I see the gentleman resembles the Major somewhat," he said.

"An amazing likeness. Now—" he stared at the ceiling. "We will begin with a very dry Madeira, I think; Sercial, the 1875. Then we will whet our appetites with *Les Huîtres de*

Whitstable, with a white Burgundy; Chablis Vaudesir. I think there is still a bit of the '29."

I leaned forward. This sounded like something special indeed. I had eaten oysters Whitstable before, but the wines were vintages of which I had only heard.

"The soup, *Consomme Double aux Cepes;* then *Le Supreme de Brochet au Beurre Blanc,* and for our first red Burgundy, Romanee-Conti, 1904."

Brion ran through the remainder of a sumptuous menu. Luc went away quietly. If he could carry that in his head, he was the kind of waiter I'd always wanted to find.

"Luc has been with me for many years," Brion said. "A faithful friend. You noticed that he called me 'Major.' That was the last official rank I held in the Army of France-in-Exile, before the collapse. I was later elected as Colonel over a regiment of survivors of the Battle of Gibraltar when we had realized that we were on our own. Later still, when I saw what had to be done, and took into my hands the task of rebuilding, other titles were given me by my followers, and I confess I conferred one or two myself; it was a necessary psychological measure, I felt. But to Luc I have always remained 'Major.' He himself was a sons-officer, my regimental Sergeant-Major."

"I know little about events of the last few years in Europe," I said. "Can you tell me something about them?"

He sat thoughtfully for a moment. "The course was steadily downhill," he said, "from the day of the unhappy Peace of Munich in 1919. America faced the Central Powers alone, and the end was inevitable. When America fell under the massive onslaught in '32, it seemed that the Kaiser's dream of a German-dominated world was at hand. Then came the uprisings. I held a Second Lieutenant's commission in the Army of France-in-Exile. We spearheaded the organized resistance, and the movement spread like wildfire.

Men, it seemed, would not live as slaves. We had high hopes in those days.

"But the years passed, and stalemate wore away at us. At last the Kaiser was overthrown by a palace coup, and we chose that chance to make our last assault. I led my battalion on Gibraltar, and took a steel-jacketed bullet through both knees almost before we were ashore.

"I will never forget the hours of agony while I lay conscious in the surgeons' tent. There was no more morphine, and the medical officers worked over the minor cases, trying to get men back into the fight; I was out of it and therefore took last priority. It was reasonable, but at the time I did not understand."

I listened, rapt. "When," I asked, "were you hit?"

"That day I will not soon forget," he said. "April 15, 1945."

I stared. I had been hit by a German machine gun slug at Jena and had waited in the aid station for the doctors to get to me—on April 15, 1945. There was a strange affinity that linked this other Bayard's life with mine, even across the unimaginable void of the Net.

We finished the 1855 brandy, and still we sat, talking through the African night. We laid ambitious plans for the rebuilding of civilization. We enjoyed each other's company, and all stiffness had long since gone. I closed my eyes, and I think I must have dozed off. Something awakened me.

Dawn was lightening the sky. Brion sat silent, frowning. He tilted his head.

"Listen."

I listened. I thought I caught a faint shout and something banged in the distance. I looked inquiringly at my host. His face was grim.

"All is not well," he said. He gripped the chair arms, rose, got his canes, started around the table.

I got up and stepped forward through the glass doors into the room. I was dizzy from the wine and brandy. There was a louder shout outside in the hall and a muffled thump. Then the door shook, splintered and crashed inward.

Thin in a tight black uniform, Chief Inspector Bale stood in the opening, his face white with excitement. He carried a long-barreled Mauser automatic pistol in his right hand. He stared at me, stepped back, then with a sudden grimace raised the gun and fired.

In the instant before the gun slammed, I caught a blur of motion from my right, and then Brion was there, half in front of me, falling as the shot echoed. I grabbed for him, caught him by the shoulders as he went down, limp. Blood welled from under his collar, spreading; too much blood, a life's blood. He was looking into my face as the light died from his eyes.

CHAPTER THIRTEEN

"GET BACK, Bayard," Bale snarled. "Rotten luck, that; I needed the swine alive for hanging." I stood up slowly. He stared at me, gnawing his lip. "It was you I wanted dead; and this fool traded lives with you."

He seemed to be talking to himself. I recognized the voice now, a little late. Bale was the Big Boss. It was the fact that he spoke in French here that had fooled me.

"All right," he said in abrupt decision. "He can trade deaths with you too. You'll do to hang in his place. I'll give the mob their circus. You wanted to take his place, here's your chance.

He stepped farther into the room, motioned others in. Evil-looking thugs came through the door, peering about, glancing at Bale for orders.

"Put him in a cell," Bale said. "And I'm warning you, Cassu, keep your bloody hands off him. I want him strong for the surgeon."

Cassu grunted, twisted my arm until the joint creaked, and pushed me past the dead body of the man I had come in one night to think of as a brother.

They marched me off down the corridor, pushed me into an elevator, led me out again through a mob of noisy toughs armed to the teeth, down stone stairs, along a damp tunnel in the rock, and at the end of the line, sent me spinning with a kick into the pitch black of a cell.

My stunned mind worked, trying to assimilate what had happened. Bale! And not a double; he had known who I was. It was Bale of the Imperium, a traitor. That answered a lot of questions. It explained the perfect timing and placement of the attack at the palace, and why Bale had been too busy to attend the gala affair that night. I realized now why he had sought me out afterward; he was hoping that I'd been killed, of course. That would have simplified matters for him. And the duel—I had never quite been able to understand why the Intelligence chief had been willing to risk killing me, when I was essential to the scheme for controlling the dictator. And all the lies about the viciousness of the Bayard of B-I Two were Bale's fabrications designed to prevent establishment of friendly relations between the Imperium and this unhappy world.

Why? I asked myself. Did Bale plan to rule this hell-world himself, making it his private domain? It seemed so.

And I saw that Bale did not intend to content himself with this world alone; this would be merely a base of operations, a source of fighting men and weapons—including atomic bombs. Bale himself was the author of the raids on the Imperium. He had stolen shuttles, or components thereof, and had manned them here in B-I Two, and set out on a career of piracy. The next step would be the assault on the Imperium itself, a full-scale attack, strewing atomic death. The men of the Imperium would wear gay uniforms and dress sabres into battle against atomic cannon.

I wondered why I hadn't realized it sooner. The fantastic unlikeliness of the development of the MC drive independently by the war-ruined world of B-I Two seemed obvious now.

While we had sat in solemn conference, planning moves against the raiders, their prime mover had sat with us. No wonder an enemy scout had lain in wait for me as I came in on my mission.

When he found me at the hideout, Bale must have immediately set to work planning how best to make use of the unexpected stroke of luck. And when I had escaped, he had had to move fast.

I could only assume that the State was now in his hands; that a show execution of Bayard in the morning had been scheduled to impress the populace with the reality of the change in regimes.

Now I would hang in the dictator's place. And I remembered what Bale had said: he wanted me strong for the surgeon. The wash tub would be useful after all. There were enough that knew the dictator's secret to make a corpse with legs embarrassing.

They would shoot me full of dope, perform the operation, bind up the stumps, dress my unconscious body in a uniform and hang me. A dead body wouldn't fool the public. They would be able to see the color of life in my face, even if I were still out, as the noose tightened.

I heard someone coming, and saw a bobbing light in the passage through the barred opening in the door. I braced myself. Maybe this was the man with the saws and the heavy snippers already.

Two men stopped at the cell door, opened it, came in. I squinted at the glare of the flashlight. One of the two dropped something on the floor.

"Put it on," he said. "The boss said he wanted you should wear this here for the hanging."

I saw my old costume, the one I had washed. At least it was clean, I thought. It was strange, I considered, how inconsequentials still had importance.

A foot nudged me. "Put it on, like I said."

"Yeah," I said. I took off the robe and pulled on the light wool jacket and trousers, buckled the belt. There were no shoes; I guessed Bale figured I wouldn't be needing them.

"OK," the man said. "Let's go, Hiem."

I sat and listened as the door clanked again; the light receded. It was very dark.

I fingered the torn lapels of my jacket. The communicator hadn't helped me much. I could feel the broken wires, tiny filaments projecting from the cut edge of the cloth. Beau Joe had cursed as he slashed at them!

I looked down. Tiny blue sparks jumped against the utter black as the wires touched.

I sat perfectly still. Sweat broke out on my forehead. I didn't dare move; the pain of hope awakening against all hope was worse then the blank acceptance of certain death.

My hands shook. I fumbled for the wires, tapped them together. A spark; another.

I tried to think. The communicator was clipped to my belt still; the speaker and mike were gone but the power source was there. Was there a possibility that touching the wires together would transmit a signal? I didn't know. I could only try.

I didn't know Morse Code, or any other code; but I knew S.O.S. Three dots, three dashes, three dots. Over and over, while I suffered the agony of hope.

A long time passed. I tapped the wires, and waited. I almost fell off the bunk as I dozed for an instant. I couldn't stop; I had to try until time ran out for me.

I heard them coming from far off, the first faint grate of leather on dusty stone, a clink of metal. My mouth was dry, and my legs began to tingle. I thought of the hollow tooth and ran my tongue over it. The time for it had come. I wondered how it would taste, if it would be painful. I wondered if Bale had forgotten it, or if he hadn't known.

There were more sounds in the passage now, sounds of men and loud voices; a clank of something heavy, a ponderous grinding. They must be planning on setting the table up here in the cell, I thought. I went to the tiny opening in the door and looked through. I could see nothing but almost total darkness. Suddenly light flared brilliantly, and I jumped, blinded.

There was more noise, then someone yelled. They must be having a hell of a time getting the stuff through the narrow hall, I thought. My eyeballs ached, my legs were trembling, my stomach suddenly felt bad. I gagged. I hoped I wouldn't go to pieces. Time for the tooth now. I thought of how disappointed Bale would be when he found me dead in my cell. It helped a little; but still I hesitated. I didn't want to die. I had a lot of living I wanted to do first.

Then someone called out, nearby.

"Wolfhound!"

My head came up. My code-name. I tried to shout, choked.

"Yes," I croaked. I jumped to the bars, yelled.

"Wolfhound, where in hell…"

"Here!" I yelled. "Here!"

"Get back, Colonel," someone said. "Get in the corner and cover up."

I moved back and crouched, arms over my head. There was a sharp hissing sound, and a mighty blast that jarred the floor under me. Tiny particles bit and stung, and grit was in my mouth. With a drawn-out clang, the door fell into the room.

Arms grabbed me, pulled me through the boiling dust, out into the glare. I stumbled, felt broken things underfoot.

Men milled around a mass blocking the passage. Canted against the wall a great box sat with a door hanging wide, light streaming out. Arms helped me through the door, and I saw wires, coils, junction boxes, stapled to bare new wood, with angle irons here and there. White-uniformed men crowded into the tiny space; a limp figure was hauled through the door.

"Full count," someone yelled. "Button up!" Wood splintered as a bullet came through.

The door banged shut, and the box trembled while a rumble built up into a whine, then passed on up out of audibility.

Someone grabbed my arm. "My God, Brion, you must have had a terrible time of it."

It was Richthofen, in a grey uniform, a cut on his face, staring at me.

"No hard feelings," I said. "Your timing...was good."

"We've had a monitor on your band day and night, hoping for something," he said. "We'd given you up, but couldn't bring ourselves to abandon hope; then four hours ago the tapping started coming through. They went after it with locators, and fixed it here in the wine cellars.

"The patrol scouts couldn't get in here; no room. We pitched this box together and came in."

"Fast work," I said. I thought of the trip through the dreaded Blight, in a jury-rig made of pine boards. I felt a certain pride in the men of the Imperium.

"Make a place for Colonel Bayard, men," someone said. A space was cleared on the floor, jackets laid out on it. Richthofen was holding me up and I made a mighty effort, got to the pallet and collapsed. Richthofen said something but I didn't hear it. I wondered what had held the meat cutters up so long, and then let it go. I had to say something, warn them. I couldn't remember...

CHAPTER FOURTEEN

I WAS lying in a clean bed in a sunny room, propped up on pillows. It was a little like another room I had awakened in not so long before, but there was one important difference. Barbro sat beside my bed, knitting a ski stocking from red wool. Her hair was piled high on her head, and the sun shone through it, coppery red. Her eyes were hazel, and her features were perfect, and I liked lying there looking at her. She had come every day since my return to the Imperium, and read to me, talked to me, fed me soup and fluffed my pillows. I was enjoying my convalescence.

"If you are good, Brion," Barbro said, "and eat all of your soup today, perhaps by tomorrow evening you will be strong enough to accept the king's invitation."

"OK," I said. "It's a deal."

"The Emperor Ball," Barbro said, "is the most brilliant affair of the year and all the three kings and the Emperor with their ladies will be there together."

I didn't answer; I was thinking. There seemed to be something I wasn't figuring out. I had been leaving all the problems to the Intelligence men, but I knew more than they did about Bale.

I thought of the last big affair, and the brutal attack. I suspected that this time every man would wear a slug-gun under his braided cuff. But the fight on the floor had been merely a diversion, designed to allow the crew to set up an atomic bomb.

I sat bolt upright. That bomb had been turned over to Bale. There would be no chance of surprise attack from a shuttle this time, with alert crews watching around the clock for traces of unscheduled ME activity; but there was no need to bring a bomb in. Bale had one here.

"What is it, Brion?" Barbro asked, leaning forward.

"What did Bale do with that bomb?" I said. "The one they tried to set off at the dance. Where is it now?"

"I don't know. It was turned over to Inspector Bale..."

"When do the royal parties arrive for the Emperor Ball?" I asked.

"They are already in the city," Barbro said, "at Drottningholm."

I felt my heart start to beat a little faster. Bale wouldn't let this opportunity pass. With the three kings here in the city, and an atomic bomb hidden somewhere, he had to act. At one stroke he could wipe out the leadership of the Imperium, and follow-up with a full-scale assault; and against his atomic weapons, the fight would be hopeless.

"Call Manfred, Barbro," I said. "Tell him that bomb's got to be found fast. The kings will have to be evacuated from the city; the ball will have to be cancelled..."

Barbro spoke into the phone, looked back at me. "He has left the building, Brion," she said. "Shall I try to reach Herr Goering?"

"Yes," I said. I started to tell her to hurry, but she was already speaking rapidly to someone at Goering's office. Barbro was quick to catch on.

"He also is out," Barbro said. "Is there anyone else?"

I thought furiously. Manfred or Hermann would listen to anything I might say, but with their staffs it would be a different matter. To call off the day of celebration, disturb the royal parties, alarm the city, were serious measures. No one would act on my vague suspicions alone. I had to find my friends in a hurry—or find Bale.

Imperial Intelligence had made a search, found nothing. His apartment was deserted, as well as his small house at the edge of the city. And the monitors had detected no shuttle not known to be an Imperium vessel moving in the Net recently.

There were several possibilities; one was that Bale had returned almost at the same time as I had, slipping in before the situation was known, while some of his own men still manned the alert stations. A second was that he planned to come in prepared to hold off attackers until he could detonate the bomb. Or possibly an accomplice would act for him.

Somehow I liked the first thought best. It seemed more in keeping with what I knew of Bale; shrewder, less dangerous. If I were right, Bale was here now, somewhere in Stockholm, waiting for the hour to blow the city sky-high.

As for the hour, he would wait for the arrival of the Emperor, not longer.

"Barbro," I said, "when does the Emperor arrive?"

"I'm not sure, Brion," she said. "Possibly tonight, but perhaps this afternoon."

That didn't give me much time. I jumped out of bed, and staggered.

"Here I come, ready or not," I said. "I can't just lie here, Barbro. Do you have a car?"

"Yes, my car is downstairs, Brion. Sit down and let me help you." She went to the closet and I sank down. I seemed always to be recuperating lately. I had been through this shaky-legs business just a few days ago, and here I was starting in again. Barbro turned, holding a brown suit in her hands.

"This is all there is, Brion," she said. "It is the uniform of the dictator, that you wore when you came here to the hospital."

"It will have to do," I said. Barbro helped me dress, and we left the room as fast as I could walk. A passing nurse stared, but went on. I was dizzy and panting already.

The elevator helped. I sank down on the stool, head spinning.

I felt something stiff in my chest pocket, and suddenly I had a vivid recollection of Gaston giving me a card as we crouched in the dusk behind the hideout near Algiers, telling me that he thought it was the address of the Big Boss's out-of-town headquarters. I grabbed for the card, squinted at it in the dim light of the ceiling lamp as the car jolted to a stop.

"Ostermalmsgatan 71" was scrawled across the card in blurred pencil. I remembered how I had dismissed it from my mind as of no interest when Gaston had handed it to me; I had hoped for something more useful. Now this might be the little key that could save an empire.

"What is it, Brion?" Barbro asked. "Have you found something?"

"I don't know," I said. "Maybe just a dead end, but maybe not." I handed her the card. "Do you know where this is?"

She read the address. "I think I know the street," she said. "It is not far from the docks, in the warehouse district."

"Let's go," I said, with a fervent hope that we were right, and not too late.

We squealed around a corner, slowed in a street of gloomy warehouses, blind glass windows in looming brick-red facades, with yard-high letters identifying the shipping lines, which owned them.

"This is the street," Barbro said. "And the number was seventy-one?"

"That's right," I said. "This is seventy-three; stop here."

We stepped out onto a gritty sidewalk, shaded by the bulk of the buildings, silent. There was a smell of tar and hemp in the air and a hint of seawater.

I stared at the building before me. There was a small door set in the front beside a loading platform. I went up to it, tried it. Locked. I leaned against it and rested.

"Barbro," I said. "Get me a jack handle or tire tool from your car." I hated to drag Barbro into this, but I had no choice. I couldn't do it alone.

She came back with a flat piece of steel eighteen inches long. I jammed it into the wide crack at the edge of the door and pulled. Something snapped, and with a jerk the door popped open. A stair ran up into gloom above. Barbro gave me an arm, and we started up. The hard work helped to keep my mind off the second sun that might light the Stockholm sky at any moment.

Five flights up, we reached a landing. The door we faced was of red-stained wood, solid and with a new lock. I looked at the hinge pins. They didn't look as good as the lock.

It took fifteen minutes, every one of which took a year off my life, but after a final wrench with the steel bar, the last pin clattered to the floor. The door pivoted out and fell against the wall.

"Wait here," I said. I started forward, into the papered hall.

"I'm going with you, Brion," Barbro said. I didn't argue.

We were in a handsome apartment, a little too lavishly furnished. Persian rugs graced the floor, and in the bars of dusty sunlight that slanted through shuttered windows, mellow old teak furniture gleamed, and polished ivory figurines stood on dark shelves under silk scrolls from Japan.

An ornate screen stood in the center of the room. I walked around a brocaded ottoman over to the screen and looked behind it. On a light tripod of aluminum rods rested the bomb.

Two heavy castings, bolted together around a central flange, with a few wires running along to a small metal box on the underside. Midway up the curve of the side, four small holes, arranged in a square. That was all there was; but it could make a mighty crater where a city had been.

I had no way of knowing whether it was armed or not. I leaned toward the thing, listening. I could hear no sound of a timing device. I thought of cutting the exposed wires, which looked like some sort of jury-rig, but I couldn't risk it; that might set it off.

"Here it is," I said, "but when does it go up?" I had an odd sensation of intangibility, as though I were already a puff of incandescent gas. I tried to think.

"Start searching the place, Barbro," I said. "You might come across something that will give us a hint. I'll phone Manfred's office and get a squad up here to see if we can move the thing without blowing it."

I dialed Imperial Intelligence. Manfred wasn't in, and the fellow on the phone was uncertain what he should do.

"Get a crew here on the double," I yelled. "Somebody who can at least make a guess as to whether this thing can be disturbed."

He said he would confer with General Somebody.

"When does the Emperor arrive?" I asked him. He was sorry, but he was not at liberty to discuss the Emperor's movements. I slammed the receiver down.

"Brion," Barbro called. "Look what's here."

I went to the door, which opened onto the next room. A two-man shuttle filled the space. Its door stood open. I looked inside. It was fitted out in luxury; Bale provided well for himself even for short trips. This was what he used to travel from the home line to B-I Two. And the fact that it was here should indicate that Bale was here also; and that he would return to it before the bomb went off.

But then again, perhaps the bomb was even now ticking away its last seconds, and Bale might be far away, safe from the blast. If the latter were true, there was nothing I could do about it; but if he did plan to return here, arm the bomb, set a timer and leave via the shuttle in the bedroom—then maybe I could stop him.

"Barbro," I said, "you've got to find Manfred or Hermann. I'm going to stay here and wait for Bale to come back. If you find them, tell them to get men here fast who can make a try at disarming this thing. I don't dare move it, and it will take at least two to handle it. If we can move it, we can shove it in the shuttle and send it off; I'll keep phoning. I don't know where you should look but do your best."

Barbro looked at me. "I would rather stay here with you, Brion," she said. "But I understand that I must not."

"You're quite a girl, Barbro," I said.

CHAPTER FIFTEEN

I WAS alone now, except for the ominous sphere behind the screen. I hoped for a caller, though. I went to the door, which leaned aslant against the rough brick wall outside and unlatched it, maneuvered it into place and dropped the pins back in the hinges, then closed and relatched it.

I went back to the over-stuffed room, started looking through drawers, rifling through papers on the desk. I hoped for something—something that might give me a hint of what Bale planned. I didn't find any hints, but I did find a long-barreled twenty-two revolver, loaded. That helped. I hadn't given much thought to what I would do when Bale got here. I was in no condition to grapple with him; now I had a reasonable chance.

I picked out a hiding place to duck into when and if I heard him coming, a storeroom in the hall, between the bomb and the door. I found a small liquor cabinet and poured myself two fingers of sherry.

I sat in one of the fancy chairs, and tried to let myself go limp. I was using up too much energy in tension. My stomach was a hard knot. I could see the edge of the bomb behind its screen from where I sat. I wondered if there would be any warning before it detonated. My ears were cocked for a click or a rumble from the silent grey city-killer.

The sound I heard was not a click; it was the scrape of shoes on wood, beyond the door. I sat paralyzed for a moment, then got to my feet, stepped to the storeroom and eased behind the door. I loosened the revolver in my pocket and waited.

The sounds were closer now, gratingly loud in the dead silence. Then a key scraped in the lock, and a moment later the tall thin figure of Chief Inspector Bale, traitor, shuffled into view. His small bald head was drawn down between his shoulders, and he looked around the room almost furtively. He pulled off his coat, and for one startled instant I thought he would come to my storeroom to hang it up; but he threw it over the back of a chair.

He went to the screen, peered at the bomb. I could easily have shot him, but that wouldn't have helped me. I wanted Bale to let me know whether the bomb was armed, if it could be moved. He was the only man in the Imperium who knew how to handle this device.

He leaned over the bomb, took a small box from his pocket and stared at it. He looked at his watch, went to the phone. I could barely hear his mutter as he exchanged a few words with someone. He went into the next room, and as I was about to follow to prevent his using the shuttle, he came back. He looked at his watch again, sat in a chair, and opened a small tool kit, which lay on the table. He started to work on the metal box with a slender screwdriver. This, then, was the arming device. I tried not to breathe too loud, or to think about how my legs ached.

Shocking in the stillness, the phone rang. Bale looked up, startled, laid the screwdriver and the box on the table, and went over to the phone. He looked down at it, chewing his lip. After five rings it stopped. I wondered who it was.

Bale went back to his work. Now he was replacing the cover on the box, frowning over the job. He got up, went to the bomb, licked his lips and leaned over it. He was ready now to arm the bomb. I couldn't wait any longer.

I pushed the door open, and Bale leaped upright, grabbing for his chest, then jumped for the coat on the chair.

"Stand where you are, Bale," I said. "I'd get a real kick out of shooting you."

Bale's eyes were almost popping from his head, his head was tilted back, his mouth opened and closed. I got the impression that I had startled him.

"Sit down," I said. "There." I motioned with the pistol as I came out into the room.

"Bayard," Bale said hoarsely. I didn't say anything. I felt sure now that the bomb was safe. All I had to do was wait until the crew arrived and turn Bale over to them. Then we could carry the bomb to the shuttle, and send it off into the Blight. But I was feeling very bad now.

I went to a chair, and sank down. I tried not to let Bale see how weak I was. I leaned back, and tried breathing deep through my nose again. If I started to pass out I would have to shoot Bale; he couldn't be left free to threaten the Imperium again.

It was little better now. Bale stood rigid, staring at me.

"Look, Bayard," he said. "I'll bring you in on this with me. I swear I'll give you a full half share. I'll let you keep B-I Two as your own, and I shall take the home line; there's plenty for all. Just put that gun aside..." He licked his lips, started towards me.

I started to motion with the gun, squeezed the trigger instead. A bullet slapped Bale's shirtsleeve, smacked the wall. He dropped down into the chair behind him. That was close, I thought. That could have killed him. I've got to hold on.

I might as well impress him a little, I thought. "I know how to use this pop gun, you see," I said. "Just a quarter of an inch from the arm, firing from the hip; not bad, don't you agree? Don't try anything else."

"You've got to listen to me, Bayard," Bale said. "Why should you care what happens to these popinjays? We can rule as absolute monarchs."

Bale went on, but I wasn't listening. I was concentrating on staying conscious, waiting for the sounds of help arriving.

"...take one moment, and we're off. What about it?"

Bale was looking at me, with a look of naked greed. I didn't know what he had been saying. He must have interpreted my silence as weakness; he got up again, moved toward me. It was darker in the room; I rubbed my eyes. I was feeling very bad now, very weak. My heart thumped in my throat, my stomach quivered. I was in no shape to be trying to hold this situation in check alone.

Bale stopped, and I saw that he suddenly realized that I was blacking out. He crouched, and with a snarl jumped at me. I would have to kill him. I fired the pistol twice, and Bale reeled away, startled, but still standing.

"Hold on, Bayard, for the love of God," he squealed.

I was still alive enough to kill him. I raised the pistol, aimed and fired. I saw a picture jump on the wall. Bale leaped aside. I didn't know if I had hit him yet or not. I was losing my hold, but I wouldn't let him get away. I fired twice more, peering from my chair, and I knew it was the light in my mind fading, not in the room. Bale yelled; I saw that he didn't dare to try for the door to the hall or the room where the shuttle waited. He would have to pass me. He screamed as I aimed the pistol with wavering hands, and dived for the other door. I fired and heard the sound echo through a dream of blackness.

I wasn't out for more than a few minutes; I came to myself, sitting in the chair, the pistol lying on my lap. The screen had fallen over, and lay across the bomb. I sat up, panicky; maybe Bale had armed it. And where was Bale? I remembered only that he had dashed for the next room. I got up, grabbed for the chair again, then got my balance, made my way to the door. There was a strange sound, a keening, like a cat in the distant alley. I looked into the room, half expecting to see Bale lying on the floor. There was nothing. The light streamed through an open window, and a curtain flapped. Bale must have panicked and jumped, I thought. I went to the window, and the keening started up again.

Bale hung by his hands from the eave of the building across the alley, fifteen feet away. The sound came from him. The left leg of his trousers had a long stain of blackish red on it, and drops fell from the toe of his shoe, five stories to the brick pavement below.

"Good God, Bale," I said. "What have you done?" I was horrified. I had been ready to shoot him down, but to see him hanging there was something else again.

"Bayard," he croaked, "I can't hold on much longer. For the love of God..."

What could I do? I was far too weak for any heroics. I looked around the room frantically for an inspiration; I needed a plank or a piece of rope. There was nothing. I pulled a sheet off the bed; it was far too short. Even two or three would never make it. And I couldn't hold it even if I could throw it and Bale caught it. I ran to the phone.

"Operator," I called. "There's a man about to fall from a roof. Get the fire department here with ladders, fast; seventy-one Ostermalmsgatan, fifth floor."

I dropped the phone, ran back to the window. "Hold on, Bale," I said. "Help's on the way." He must have tried to leap to the next roof, thinking that I was at his heels; and with that hole in his leg he hadn't quite made it.

I thought of Bale, sending me off on a suicide mission, knowing that my imposture was hopeless as long as I stood on my own legs; I thought of the killer shuttle that had lain in wait to smash us as we went in; of the operating room at the hideout, where Bale had planned to carve me into a shape more suitable for his purpose. I remembered Bale shooting down my newfound brother, and the night I had lain in the cold cell, waiting for the butcher; and still I didn't want to see him die this way.

He started to scream suddenly, kicking desperately. He got one foot up on the eave beside his white straining hands; it slipped off. Then he was quiet again. I had been standing here now for five minutes. I wondered how long I had been unconscious. Bale had been there longer now than I would have thought possible. He couldn't last much longer.

"Hold on, Bale," I called. "Only a little while. Don't struggle."

He hung, silent. Blood dripped from his shoe. I looked down at the alley below and shuddered.

I heard a distant sound, a siren, howling. I dashed to the door, opened it, listened. Heavy footsteps sounded below.

"Here," I shouted, "all the way up."

I turned and ran back to the window. Bale was as I had left him. Then one hand slipped off, and he hung by one arm, swinging slightly.

"They're here, Bale," I said. "A few seconds…"

He didn't try to get a new hold. He made no sound. Feet pounded on the stairs outside and I yelled again.

I turned back to the window as Bale slipped down, silent. I didn't watch. I heard him hit—twice.

I staggered back, and the burly men called, looked out the window, milled about. I made my way back to the chair, slumped down. I was empty of emotion. There was noise all around me, people coming and going. I was hardly conscious of it. After a long time I saw Hermann, and then Barbro was leaning over me. I reached for her hand, hungrily.

"Take me home, Barbro," I said.

I saw Manfred.

"The bomb," I said. "It's safe. Put it in the shuttle and get rid of it."

"My crew is moving it now, Brion," he said.

"You spoke of home, just now," Goering put in. "Speaking for myself, and I am sure also for Manfred, I will make the strongest recommendation that in view of your extraordinary services to the Imperium you be dispatched back to your home as soon as you are well enough to go, if that is your wish. I hope that you will stay with us. But it must be for you to make that decision."

"I don't have to decide," I said. "My choice is made. I like it here, for many reasons. For one thing, I can use all the old cliches from B-I Three, and they sound brand new; and as for home…" I looked at Barbro:

"Home is where the heart is."

THE END

If you've enjoyed this book, you will not want to miss these terrific titles…

ARMCHAIR SCI-FI & HORROR DOUBLE NOVELS, $12.95 each

D-51   **A GOD NAMED SMITH** by Henry Slesar
         WORLDS OF THE IMPERIUM by Keith Laumer

D-52   **CRAIG'S BOOK** by Don Wilcox
         EDGE OF THE KNIFE by H. Beam Piper

D-53   **THE SHINING CITY** by Rena M. Vale
         THE RED PLANET by Russ Winterbotham

D-54   **THE MAN WHO LIVED TWICE** by Rog Phillips
         VALLEY OF THE CROEN by Lee Tarbell

D-55   **OPERATION DISASTER** by Milton Lesser
         LAND OF THE DAMNED by Berkeley Livingston

D-56   **CAPTIVE OF THE CENTAURIANESS** by Poul Anderson
         A PRINCESS OF MARS by Edgar Rice Burroughs

D-57   **THE NON-STATISTICAL MAN** by Raymond F. Jones
         MISSION FROM MARS by Rick Conroy

D-58   **INTRUDERS FROM THE STARS** by Ross Rocklynne
         FLIGHT OF THE STARLING by Chester S. Geier

D-59   **COSMIC SABOTEUR** by Frank M. Robinson
         LOOK TO THE STARS by Willard Hawkins

D-60   **THE MOON IS HELL!** by John W. Campbell, Jr.
         THE GREEN WORLD by Hal Clement

ARMCHAIR SCIENCE FICTION CLASSICS, $12.95 each

C-16   **THE SHAVER MYSTERY, Book Three**
         by Richard S. Shaver

C-17   **GIRLS FROM PLANET 5**
         by Richard Wilson

C-18   **THE FOURTH "R"**
         by George O. Smith

ARMCHAIR SCIENCE FICTION & HORROR GEMS SERIES, $12.95 each

G-5   **SCIENCE FICTION GEMS, Vol. Three**
         C. M. Kornbluth and others

G-6   **HORROR GEMS, Vol. Three**
         August Derleth and others